FOR ALL ETERNI-TEA

A PEBBLE COVE TEAHOUSE MYSTERY

ERYN SCOTT

KRISTOPHERSON PRESS

Pebble Cove will never be the same.

The Rickster is notorious for telling tall tales around Pebble Cove. When he's found on the dock holding a bloody knife, a crumpled body at his feet, of course he has a story to explain it away. But is his plea of innocence just another yarn?

The victim and the Rickster share a long history, and at the Rickster's pleading, Rosemary digs into the case. Unfortunately, the more she finds, the guiltier the man appears.

Even so, the Rickster's case brings a welcome reprieve from her other active investigation. With the help of Asher's distant, living relative, she's closing in on the truth about her ghostly friend's murder. But are Rosemary and Asher ready to say goodbye for all eternity?

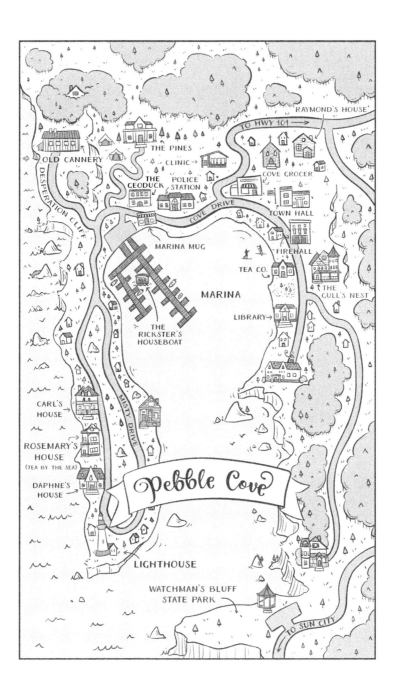

1

Laughter roared through the crowded pub as I leaned on the bar, waiting for my drink order. I made eye contact with Jimmy, the owner of the Geoduck. He chuckled and shook his head.

"For not actually being a fisherman, that guy tells the best fish stories I've ever heard," Jimmy said with a shrug.

A cool breeze rushed through the open windows, bringing much appreciated fresh air on the hot summer night.

I glanced back, only able to see wild white hair peeking out from behind a group of fishermen enraptured by the Rickster's latest story. Jimmy handed over the drinks I'd ordered. Balancing all three, I carefully picked my way back to my table.

Because of my slow pace, I overheard part of the latest story in progress as I passed by the Rickster's group.

"That's when I looked down. You know how clear the water is down in those parts," the Rickster said, pausing at just the right moment for a few of the fishermen to nod in agreement. "Well, if you haven't seen it, it's like glass that you can stick your hand right through. And that's when I saw it. Staring back at me, mere inches from my face, was a Great. White. Shark." He punctuated each word as if it were its own sentence and could stand alone.

The group of men, who had been leaning ever closer during the Rickster's story, moved back, letting out loud whoops of excitement.

"Those things are huge."

"I've seen one before."

"Oh, I have too. They're beasts."

"What did you do?"

As if he'd been waiting for that last question in order to move on, the Rickster cocked an eyebrow, his two different-colored eyes gleaming in the warm light of the pub. He had the men in the palm of his hand, just where he wanted them.

"My buddy was on the other side of the catamaran, and he chose that moment to lean all his weight onto his side—like I'd been screaming at him to do since we started tipping over—and he finally righted the boat. We moved away from the shark and sailed off to safety." The Rickster smirked, sitting back and taking a long swig of his beer.

A collective exhale left the group of fishermen. I moved past them to rejoin my friends. Jolene and Callie huddled close together over the table. The huge grins and doe-eyed expressions they wore told me exactly what they were discussing: Beck and Owen, their significant others. They sat back as I approached, clearing their throats when I set the round of drinks on the table.

"The Rickster's in fine form tonight," Jolene said, eyeing the group crowded around him in the corner.

Still standing, I took a sip of my full drink. "Shark stories always get fishermen excited. It's like hearing about the royal family, for regular people."

"Or gossiping about celebrities," Callie added.

"Did I ever tell you about the time I was shipwrecked with a Hollywood starlet?" The Rickster's crackling voice cut through the Geoduck.

The group roared with a mixture of excitement and disbelief.

Disbelief.

That was the only emotion I ever felt when the Rickster opened his mouth. But that man was part of the fabric of Pebble Cove. Everyone could recite a list of at least six unbelievable things the Rickster claimed to have happened to him—and they were usually different for each person. He had a "guy" for every situation. And we basically just tolerated him lying about his life.

He lived on a small houseboat, was always looking for the next money-making scheme to get involved in, and couldn't seem to keep his nose out of other people's business, even though he vehemently hated when people got involved in his.

Sinking into the third seat at the round table, I said, "You know you can talk about them in front of me." When my friends blinked, feigning ignorance, I clarified, "Owen and Beck. You can gush about them around me too. You don't have to wait until I'm gone."

Callie studied her drink while Jolene tugged on her ear.

Over the last few months, I'd noticed a trend. My

friends, who were both in new relationships, had been holding back around me when it came to discussing how happy they were.

"We just don't want you to feel left out." Jolene bowed her head forward. "But in trying to do so, we're *actually* leaving you out," she added, like saying it aloud had helped her understand how backward it sounded.

"We're sorry." Callie traced a meandering pathway through the condensation on her glass. "We won't hide it anymore. We promise. But you can tell us to stop if you ever feel like we're talking about them too much."

Taking another sip of my drink, I shook my head. "I doubt I'll ever feel that way. They make you happy. I'm thrilled for both of you. I mean, Jolene, you're married. That's a big deal."

Jolene and Beck had eloped during their trip to Tahiti a few months ago. He was a website designer, so he worked remotely, and he'd moved in with her once they'd come home. They were the definition of wedded bliss.

Callie and Owen weren't engaged yet, but they seemed to be perfect for each other. And even though Owen was still on the shy side, it was the thing Callie had grown to like most about him: his quiet nature.

"Speaking of relationships, though … Rosemary, what's going on with Riley?" Jolene asked, drumming her fingernails on the table expectantly.

Callie's eyes flicked to me, and then she went back to focusing on the glass in front of her. Her evident discomfort mirrored mine. My toes scrunched up in my sandals and heat crept across my chest.

"He's just a friend." My voice was tight and came out

sounding hoarse. "We're doing research on his family together."

Riley was a distant relative of the Benson family who used to own the house I lived in now. We were working together to get to the bottom of a century-old mystery: who had killed his great-great-great-grand uncle, Asher Benson.

What Riley *didn't* know was that Asher's ghost still resided in my house, and the real reason we needed to figure out who'd killed him was so his spirit could finally move on. You see, Callie and I could communicate with ghosts. We'd both had near-death experiences and enough run-ins with death afterward that we'd become mediums.

"But he's really cute." Jolene waggled her eyebrows. "Seriously, Rosemary. He seems to be kind, funny, and all the things you deserve."

I tried to meet Callie's gaze, to signal that I needed her help, but she was like a dog watching a squirrel and wouldn't look away from her drink. Callie knew the truth, that I couldn't possibly think of Riley in that way because I was already in love with someone else. The reason I couldn't tell that to Jolene was because the someone I was in love with was Asher.

Yes, the ghost. It was all very complicated.

For the two years since I moved into the beachside Victorian Asher had grown up in during the early nineteen hundreds, he and I had been solid. We were best friends. We loved spending time together and could just about read one another's minds. I loved him as a friend but knew I could never have a future with someone who was already dead.

Everything had changed a few months ago when we'd learned that certain gemstones, in the hands of spirits, could enhance their energy. The introduction of jasper meant Asher could become almost solid for a short period of time, without fading away for days or weeks like he used to when he would use up his ghostly energy.

With this newfound power, Asher had kissed me—the single best kiss of my life so far. I hadn't always been outgoing or social, so there hadn't been a ton of kisses in my life, but somehow I knew that the kiss I shared with Asher was going to be hard to beat.

Despite the sheer excellence of the kiss, we'd both quickly realized that acknowledging our love for one another would only lead to heartache, so we'd been operating in an odd limbo ever since.

Callie knew all about my dilemma, so she wasn't as baffled as the rest of the town seemed to be that Riley and I hadn't become anything more than friends.

"Riley's very nice." I nodded to Jolene. "He also recently got out of a relationship and isn't ready for anything yet." That was the easier answer. I hoped she took it.

"*Yet.*" Jolene dragged out the word, placing meaning where none was warranted.

"He's just not the one for Rosie." Callie finally jumped to my rescue, trying to shut down the conversation. When Jolene frowned, Callie changed the topic, saying, "Did you hear that Raymond's getting a motorcycle?"

Raymond Clemenson was Callie's and my adoptive father, and my mother's new husband. Because he had adopted us as adults, more as a symbol than anything, we'd had a hard time transitioning to calling him Dad, or anything similar. Raymond had been the local police chief to me for too long before he'd started seeing my mother, and it was going to take a while to change my habit of referring to him by his job title. I'd had no problem referring to Callie as my sister, since she'd already felt like one long before it was legal.

"A motorcycle?" I pursed my lips. "That's very midlife crisis of him."

Callie sputtered out a laugh. Jolene snorted into her drink.

"Kate said the timeline is suspicious, since he started talking about it the same week they met with the financial planner about retirement," Callie explained.

The two of them were still a decade out from retiring, but ever since they'd gotten married and merged their finances, they'd been trying to do more planning for their future. All three of us girls were already expecting the transition out of service to be hard on Raymond. His career defined so much of his life and his personality that we knew it was going to be difficult for him to separate from that part of himself when the time came.

"What kind of motorcycle? Sitting back?" I asked, holding my hands up near my face and miming handlebars. "Or forward?" I crouched over the table and pretended to hold on for dear life.

"Oh, I'd pay money to see him on one of those speed racers." Jolene let out a belly laugh. "I think I can see Raymond more on a cruiser, though."

Callie and I nodded our agreement.

"Wearing a pair of aviators, cruising up and down the coast." I smiled at the mental picture. "It might be an excellent hobby for him."

Jolene clicked her tongue. "If he's looking for hobbies,

he should try stand-up paddleboarding. I'm telling you, it's the most fun I've ever had."

Callie's expression flattened, and I pressed my lips into a thin line to stop from giggling.

"What?" Jolene asked, noticing the change in our demeanor.

"You and Beck *seriously* need to stop talking about stand-up paddleboarding." Callie shook her head.

Jolene's mouth fell open. "We don't talk about it that much."

A cackle burst out of me. I covered my mouth with my hand, waving the other in apology. "I'm so sorry. I didn't mean to laugh." But saying it didn't make the sensation go away, and I burst into another round of chuckles.

Callie caught it, too, because her shoulders shook. "It's literally what you talk about every time we see you, Jo. I heard you recommend it to no less than seven people the last time I worked at the tea company with you."

"And that's on top of all the times we see you and Beck actually paddleboarding around the cove," I added. "Which is yet another reminder."

"But the cove is—"

"Perfectly calm with an underlying current," Callie and I robotically repeated the phrase in unison, having heard her and Beck say the same thing many times.

"I suppose we *are* a little annoying about it." Jolene broke into a huge grin.

She chortled out a laugh that was so contagious, we had to join. We were swiping happy tears from our eyes minutes later when the Rickster finished another one of his stories. The group of fishermen who had been crowded around him dispersed, breaking off into smaller groups as they moved to different sections of the pub.

After gulping down the last bit of his beer, the Rickster exited the pub like he always did, loudly and as if we were all going to miss him greatly.

"Don't do anything I wouldn't do," he announced to the entire establishment with a salute before slipping out into the night.

Jolene ordered a basket of fries for our table, and the chatter inside the Geoduck leveled out to a quieter median now that the storyteller was gone. The sound of the water out the open windows created a peaceful backdrop to the perfect summer night.

But the tranquil atmosphere shattered as the front door of the pub slammed open. Chance, one of the fishermen on Dan's crew, stood in the doorway, his face pale and his mouth agape.

"Everything okay there, buddy?" Jimmy called from behind the bar.

Chance blinked. He pointed to the marina and then shook his head. "I think I just saw the Rickster stab a guy."

A round of rolling laughter peeled through the Geoduck at Chance's declaration.

"Good one." A chuckle puffed out of Jimmy. "Come on in. I'll get you a beer."

But Chance didn't move. "No. I'm serious. I think he *stabbed* a man. We need to call the police."

2

About half the customers inside the pub jumped to their feet, myself included. The other half stayed put, waving dismissive hands and taking another drink. They didn't believe Chance. It had to be a joke.

But an icy worry skated down my spine, in stark contrast to the muggy air crowding the bar. It pushed me forward, chasing after the rest of the patrons who were rushing to see if Chance was telling the truth.

"I'll call the chief," Jimmy said, shooting Callie and me a pointed look as we rushed past.

We needed to get down to the docks. Fast.

Spilling out into the darkness, we followed the group across the street and down to the dock. About ten people were in front of me, Callie, and Jolene as we all congregated in the space next to the Rickster's little blue houseboat, vying for a view.

But in the dark, it was just a mass of silhouettes and sharp elbows. I stood on my tiptoes, craning my neck to see what was happening. I tried leaning around a piling to get a different angle when my foot slipped.

A hand shot out and grabbed mine, pulling me back from falling into the water.

Asher, my ghostly best friend, had appeared next to my side. In the moonlight, his spirit almost glowed, reflecting the silvery light differently than it did the sunlight. He settled a hand on my waist, waiting until I was steady before discontinuing his use of ghostly energy and becoming transparent once more.

I gulped, having liked the feel of his hand on my waist a little too much.

"Thank you," I whispered, careful not to let anyone around hear me. Callie and I were the only people who could see Asher, so to everyone else, it would've seemed like I was talking to myself.

Asher dipped his head in a nod, winking in a way that told me he was watching out for me. That was the problem. He was always there for me. How could I *not* fall in love with him? He was sweet, thoughtful, a brilliant conversationalist, my perfect person. He'd just died almost a century before I was even born.

I turned my attention back to the scene in front of me.

"Everyone, clear out." Police Chief Raymond Clemenson's voice boomed through the crowd, the sheer weight of it seeming to push onlookers out of the way.

He'd gotten here fast. Then again, Mom was in Portland, visiting one of her friends, so he'd probably stayed late at the station, catching up on paperwork.

He strode past, through the walkway everyone had created as they took a step back. I used the break in the crowd to peek at the scene at the end of the dock. My eyes had adjusted to the darkness, and I could just make out the Rickster and a figure lying at his feet.

EMTs rushed by the chief and the Rickster, kneeling as they tended to the crumpled person. They rolled him over. In the moonlight, I could see a white shock of hair, much like the Rickster's, only it was cleanly combed to one side. A dark substance stained his tan jacket and the concrete dock. I gulped. That was a lot of blood.

Chief Clemenson coughed as he approached. The Rickster turned around to face the chief. The steel blade of a large knife glinted in the moonlight. Raymond Clemenson didn't even flinch, nor did he slow until he was a knife's edge away from the blade.

Eyes wide, the whites visible even in the darkness, the Rickster shook his head. "I didn't do this, Chief. I swear. I can explain."

"I saw you," Chance called from the back of the group. "I saw him," he repeated to the chief when he turned to see who was speaking. "He pulled the knife out and the guy fell over."

"Yeah, I pulled *out* the knife. That doesn't mean I put it there." The Rickster gestured wildly with the weapon.

Chief Clemenson raised a steady hand. "Rick, how about we stop waving that around."

The Rickster froze, moving the knife down by his side, then thought better of it and offered it—carefully—to the chief. Pulling out an evidence bag, the chief used it to grab the weapon, folding it over before checking with the EMTs. They shook their heads.

"Multiple stab wounds, sir. He's gone," one of them said.

Frowning down at the dead man, the chief said, "I need everyone to give us space, but first I need to know if anyone recognizes this man." His eyes pored over the crowd.

Behind him, the Rickster sheepishly raised his hand. The chief turned around, slowly.

"His name is Captain Westover," the Rickster said.

The chief crossed his arms. "He was the captain of a fishing boat?"

"No. Captain is his first name. He's my best friend." The Rickster glanced over his shoulder and winced at the body behind him. "Well, he *was* my best friend." His voice shook as he added that last part.

I think we all expected the Rickster to launch into a story, like he always did. But he just stood there in silent shock. It was the first time I'd seen the man speechless. My chest tightened with empathy for him. If that really was his best friend, he must be devastated.

"Rick, I know this is hard, but you've got a lot of explaining to do," Clemenson said, then dropped his voice lower. "We can talk somewhere else if you'd rather."

The Rickster blinked as if coming out of a hypnotic state. "No, it's okay. I can talk here." He cleared his throat. "Cap and I met in college." The Rickster's words came quickly. "We dropped out two weeks later, but technically, that's where we met." He flapped his arms in front of himself as the chief shifted his stance. "Don't worry, I'm getting to the point."

I swear I could hear the disbelief leaking from the audience as we listened.

"We dropped out of college because we got the chance to climb Mount Everest—which is where I was struck by lightning for the first time, by the way—and on that trip, our Sherpa hooked us up with his friend named Golly." The Rickster held up a finger to show he was getting to the point. "Golly took us on a sailing trip around the world, and that's where we started Sail Lite, our business, which he later renamed Cap's Sail Loft. I bowed out of the day-to-day stuff decades ago, and I haven't seen Cap for a few years until I walked up to my house tonight to find him standing at the end of the dock." The Rickster's nose twitched. "Well, wobbling might be a better name for what he was doing. He was leaning on the piling. I called his name, and he turned around. I almost didn't notice all the blood at first, in the dark like this. He was tugging at the knife, and I pulled it out. Then he collapsed."

Most of the stories that I'd heard the Rickster recount over the years were oratory journeys. His voice would raise at all the right moments, slow at others. He would pause in all the right places and speed up when things got really tense.

This story was different.

It wasn't a production. There were the same unbelievable elements, like climbing Everest and sailing around the world, but his tone was serious, sad. When he'd arrived at the part where his friend was stabbed, bleeding to death on his doorstep, his normally loud, commanding voice broke with an emotion I hadn't heard before.

Either the Rickster was telling the truth, or he was a way better actor than any of us gave him credit for.

"Regardless, I'm going to need to take you to the

station." The chief turned around. "Go home, everyone. There's nothing to see here."

The group, mostly comprised of fishermen, grumbled but dispersed. They'd be able to see the scene almost as well from their boats on the neighboring dock if they really wanted to get a better look. But from the eerie silence that fell over the group as they traveled slowly up the ramp to the boardwalk, I didn't think anyone wanted to see more evidence of the tragic end to Captain Westover, the Rickster's mysterious friend. Asher was gone when I turned to leave and followed Jolene and Callie up the ramp toward the boardwalk.

"If you didn't do this, you must've seen who did," the chief said, his deep voice audible behind us as we kept walking.

"I only saw Cap. Then again, I wasn't looking for anyone." The Rickster stumbled over his words. "It was dark."

Officer Gerard was waiting for the chief on the board-walk. She let us pass by, then lifted her chin as Chief Clemenson and the Rickster approached. "I searched down-town, sir. No one out of the ordinary."

"Psst. Rosemary. Callie." My ears perked up at the sound of my name. Callie tensed next to me.

We scanned the dark streets. Luckily, it was much easier to spot ghosts in the moonlight. To the right, down the boardwalk, closer to Jolene's tea shop, I spotted a glowing group of spirits.

I rammed my elbow into Callie. She latched on to my elbow and squeezed, letting me know she saw them too. The only problem was that Jolene was with us, and although she was a close friend, she didn't know about our ghost-seeing abilities.

"Well, we should probably get back to those fries," Callie said, maybe a little louder than she needed to, making me sure it was for my benefit. "Rosemary, you look a little pale. Why don't you take a moment by yourself before you come inside? You know, to catch your breath."

She was telling me to stay outside and get information from the ghosts while she kept an eye on Jolene inside. She was a good friend, and an even better sister.

"Right," I said. "I might, if that's okay."

Jolene and Callie nodded emphatically.

"We'll be right inside when you're ready." Jolene reached out and squeezed my hand.

Most of the fishermen who'd run out of the Geoduck with us flowed back inside, but a few must've been paid up and were calling it a night. The chief, Gerard, and the Rickster headed into the station, and the EMTs walked past with the body. I leaned on the railing overlooking the cove, pretending to catch my breath.

When the coast was clear, I wandered over to the grouping of ghosts down the boardwalk. All of them were here: Asher, Lois, Max, Tim, Genny, and even Meow, the former mayor and only feline ghost in town. I glanced behind me once more to make sure I was alone.

"That was crazy, right?" I kept my voice low, just in case there was someone lurking in the shadows who I hadn't seen at first. The thought of a murderer on the loose made the back of my neck go cold, and I was glad my ghostly friends surrounded me.

They chimed in with similar sentiments.

"So disturbing!"

"Do you believe the Rickster?"

"That poor man."

"I saw the whole thing."

My breath caught in my throat. "Wait. Who said that?" I scanned the small group.

Much like the Rickster, when the chief had asked if anyone recognized the dead man, Genny slowly raised her hand.

Genevieve had to have been in her eighties when she'd died. She looked like the quintessential grandma with her short, curly, white hair and pastel-blue dress. From what I could gather, she'd died in the last decade, but no one really knew her story because she clammed up and got defensive anytime someone talked about her death or why her spirit might be sticking around.

"You saw what happened to that man, Genny?" I asked, taking a step forward, then regretted it when she flinched and took a step back.

Her wrinkled face creased even more as she pointed over to the dock. "I mean, I saw you all race over there and talk to the Rickster. It was intense."

Hope leaked out of my tense posture, and I had to work hard to keep the disappointment from my features. "Oh, so you saw the same thing as everyone else."

She nodded, looking down at the ground. Tears dropped down her ghostly cheeks. She turned away from the group, wandering off.

"Genny, I didn't mean to—" I sighed as she continued walking. Turning to the rest of the group, I raised my palms in defeat. "You know I didn't mean to make her feel bad, right?"

Max and Tim nodded.

"She's just sensitive, that's all," Lois said, surprising me. Lois was one of the least sensitive spirits I knew, and also the least likely to be swayed by others' displays of emotion. "And she's especially sensitive when it comes to you."

Wincing, I said, "I know."

Ash grabbed on to my hand and squeezed tight. A spark passed between us just as it had on the dock, and I kept myself from glancing up at him.

"I shouldn't have snapped at her." I shook my head, wishing Callie was out here. Genny liked my adopted sister much better and tolerated her more than she did me.

It had all started when I'd asked Genny if she wanted help to research how she died, and what her unfinished business might be. That had offended her to no end because, *"Everyone loved me. I died peacefully in my sleep,"* she'd said. Since then, I could do nothing right in her eyes.

I was about to go back inside the Geoduck, sure I would only make things worse if I stayed, when Genny gasped behind me. I whirled around and found her staring down at the boardwalk.

"What is it?" I asked, racing over.

She pointed a shaking finger down at the weathered wood of the boardwalk. There was a large wet section, like someone had climbed up out of the cove, soaking wet.

"Rosie, you need to call the chief," Asher said. "He needs to see this."

Wet footprints led away from the cove, disappearing into the dark alley next to Cove Grocer.

3

Chief Clemenson scowled down at the footprints as he snapped pictures. He even followed them to the parking lot behind Wallace's grocery store, but there weren't any people or cars back there at that point of the night.

"Thank you, but you can head back inside, Rosie," he said, flicking through the shots he'd taken, zooming in on the tread visible in one of them.

I looked back at the Geoduck, my gaze landing on the police station. "Does this mean it wasn't the Rickster?" I asked.

The chief's large shoulders settled down an inch. "I don't know. We have an eyewitness to the stabbing, and we found him holding the murder weapon. I'm keeping him as long as I can before I have to charge him," he explained. "But these footprints do raise some interesting questions."

Despite the hopeful end of the chief's statement, I could only seem to focus on what he'd said prior to that: "Before I have to charge him." That didn't sound good for the Rickster.

The next morning, the news wasn't much better, and the tea shop was abuzz with speculations.

"My money's on the Rickster."

"Really? You think we've had a killer living in Pebble Cove this whole time?"

"Wouldn't be the first time."

"If anyone around here is capable, I'd say it's him."

Callie and I shared tense glances throughout the day. But no factual updates came with the gossip and speculation. By the time we closed, I knew my brain needed to switch gears from the Rickster's case to Asher's. Riley would be here any moment to look through letters with me. He had a box of letters, most addressed to Asher's sister, that we hoped might hold the key to his murder.

While Callie was in the kitchen prepping for tomorrow, Asher helped me clean up the tearoom, something else made possible by the jasper stones. We just had to make sure no customers were around. Floating dishware wasn't something a person saw every day.

I was just about to start the dishwasher that I'd had installed behind the tea bar when I did one last sweep of the room with my eyes.

"Ash, can you hand me that cup right there?" I pointed to a lone teacup left on a table.

But Asher didn't move. He stood there, frozen, as if he'd seen a ghost.

"Did you just call me Ash?"

It was then that I noticed the box of letters he'd placed on the table next to him and the "real Asher" standing awkwardly at the other end of the room. We shared a wide-eyed, terrified look. It was a good thing Asher hadn't been carrying a teacup at that moment, or Riley would've gotten the shock of his life.

Riley hooked a thumb behind him at the back door that led in from the deck. "The front door was locked, so I walked around and let myself in this way."

Between him showing up in a different location than I expected and the outfit he was wearing, I'd totally mistaken him for Asher.

My face heated. "Uh, yeah," I scoffed, gesturing to his outfit. "With those suspenders and the button up, you could be from the nineteen twenties." I laughed. "I called you Ash … to point that out." I pressed my lips together to stop myself from explaining any more, knowing I was just digging myself into a deeper hole.

Asher pressed his fingers to his temple and closed his eyes, unable to watch me crash and burn.

"Funny, Rosie," Riley said sarcastically, adding a charitable chuckle at the end. "But you're not the first one today to make fun of my outfit," Riley said, surveying his clothing. "My students said I was dressed like a 'total hipster,'" he explained.

While he taught courses at an online university, he often met up with his students on video calls to help them with their coursework.

I forced out a laugh. "Sounds like you've got some observant students this quarter. Should we get to work?" I motioned to the large table in the tearoom where we'd been parsing through the letters.

Asher gave me a quick salute. He'd been making himself scarce during the times Riley and I had been researching. To be honest, I think it had more to do with not being able to see me and Riley together rather than the content of the letters being too much for him. Like the rest of Pebble Cove, Asher was under the impression Riley and I would be a great match. As much as it seemed to hurt him to think about, I knew he wanted me to be happy, especially once he was gone.

Whatever the reason, I was glad he wasn't around during our research, just in case we stumbled upon something important. At that point in my life, I'd experienced quite a few spirits moving on once their unfinished business was resolved. It was an incredibly quick and final event, with little time to say goodbyes. My greatest fear was Asher disappearing from my life without us having the time to say a proper, forever kind of farewell.

Riley and I sat down, getting to work as Asher left us to it.

An hour later, however, I kind of wished Asher *had* stuck around. I wanted to hear what he'd thought of this Catherine person when he'd been alive. So far, there had been nothing in the letters that told us anything about Asher's death. They were mostly about day-to-day issues and gossip. Ninety percent of them were from a woman named Catherine. She and Hannah had kept in touch for close to a decade after Asher's family moved up to Astoria.

Catherine's handwriting, a slanted cursive that I swear got thinner each time I opened a new letter, made it difficult to skim. We had to read each one carefully.

I blinked, refocusing on the letter in front of me. I'd caught myself staring out at the water instead of reading like I was supposed to. The ocean was so calm, like shimmering glass today instead of its usual churning, crashing self. One or two lazy, rolling waves broke every few seconds. There was barely any wind, which was probably why. Because of that, it was hot. I longed to go splash around in the few small waves that were out there. Anything but this.

Riley groaned, proving I wasn't the only one growing tired of Catherine.

"She's so mean to Laura," Riley said, squeezing his eyes closed for a moment.

"Tell me about it." I snorted. "This one is all about how Laura's dress at church was raggedy and how Catherine is sure she caught Laura's husband, William, staring at her instead of his wife."

These were the parts of the letters we didn't care about. What we searched for were the sections where she responded to things Hannah had brought up in her letters to Catherine.

It was an odd form of decoding, figuring out what Hannah had probably written based on what Catherine said in response. Sometimes Catherine was a gem and repeated the question or phrase. *Georgina really said your family was a scourge on the town?* Most of the time, she wasn't so helpful, and we had to talk through the sentence to uncover the things Hannah could've written to elicit such a response. For a good portion of those instances, we were at a loss.

"I think Catherine's talking about Asher in this one." Riley sat up straight.

I set down the letter I was reading about Catherine's children. Riley read out loud, as was our custom whenever there was anything we needed to share.

"I'm so sorry that Ian is unhappy at work," Riley read. "Your father should have given him control of the business.

I am positive it would not be in this state if Ian was in charge. I am pleased to hear that your family friend will be taking the lead from this point forward. I regret I was never able to meet Charlie during the times he stayed with your family. However, I know how much of a comfort he was for you after Asher left." Riley's eyes moved right and left across the page as he read on in his head.

I was about to ask him if there was anything else, but movement in the corner of the room caught my eye. Asher stood there, frozen.

Because Asher had been killed right around when he was supposed to deploy for the front lines of World War I and his body hadn't been discovered until recently, his family thought he'd deserted. That was what Catherine had meant when she'd written "Asher left."

Hearing about how his family thought he'd deserted had to be hard on Asher. My lips parted. I wanted so badly to console Ash, to apologize that he had to hear that, but I couldn't with Riley sitting here. As I studied Ash, however, I realized he didn't appear to be devastated, like I'd expected. In fact, he looked more thoughtful than anything else.

"Charlie took over the Benson Fishing Company?" Asher's tone lilted up contemplatively. He wandered over, sinking into the chair next to me. His mouth tipped up into a tentative smile. "He *was* a good friend. I just feel sad he got dragged into all of my family's mess."

Riley stopped reading. "There's nothing else about Asher after that." He shook his head. "I wonder who this Charlie person was."

I had never heard of a Charlie either.

"Charlie McBride," Asher said. "I met him in the army.

We were in training together. He didn't have any family, so he came home with me on the breaks. He was a solid guy. Closest thing I had to a brother."

I repeated the information from Asher to Riley, adding, "Oh, I read about him in one of the journal entries from Abigail." I waved a hand dismissively, hoping Riley didn't ask to see Asher's ex-fiancée's diary because there wouldn't be anything about Charlie inside.

Riley stretched his shoulders back. "Well, it sounds like we should dig more into the person who tanked the business before this Charlie guy had to come in and take over. That person might've had a motive to get Asher out of the way, since Asher was the one who would inherit the company from his father."

Until a few months ago, we'd assumed that Asher's brother-in-law had taken over the Benson Fishing Company after Asher died and they moved the company to Astoria. He'd been the owner close to a decade later when the company went bankrupt. But it turned out that someone outside the family had owned and run the company in between those two events, and it was clear from Catherine's letter that this mystery person had been a big part of the reason the company went under.

Riley was right. Control over the Benson Fishing Company, a powerhouse business back in the early nineteen hundreds, would've definitely been a motive for murder.

"I think that's enough for today, don't you?" Nervousness crept into my tone. But I couldn't help it.

Having Asher this close to a box of evidence from the past put me on edge. What Riley had just read proved that as much as it sometimes seemed like we wouldn't learn anything more than why Catherine hated her neighbors, any of these letters could hold the answer to Asher's murder. I couldn't risk having him around when I learned the truth. I needed to savor our last days together, to tell Asher what he truly meant to me.

Sensing I was anxious, Asher reached under the table and placed a hand over mine where it sat on my bouncing leg. I shot him a grateful look out of the corner of my eye.

"Yeah, sounds good." Riley stood, gathering the letters back into the box, keeping the ones we'd already read separate from the ones we hadn't. "Same time next week?"

"Sounds good to me." I placed my hands on the table and pushed myself up.

We'd been a little ambitious at first, trying to meet multiple times in one week. But Riley's work schedule had increased with the addition of a new class he was teaching in the summer quarter. Scaling back our research to one session a week had been much more manageable for both of us.

Fridays worked best for Riley's class schedule, so we'd settled on that since he was usually the one to travel. It meant that we were going at a slower pace through the box of letters, but as long as Asher didn't seem to be in a rush, I was happy stealing as much extra time with him as I could.

When I returned from walking Riley out to his car, I found Asher in the library, staring out at the water.

"Ash, I'm sorry you had to hear that," I said, wishing I could lean my head on his shoulder.

I mean, I could—with the jasper rocks and Asher's continued practice with his energy, he could make himself solid when he needed to—but it seemed like too intimate of a gesture. Anytime he was close, all I wanted was for him to wrap his arms around me and repeat the kiss we'd shared months ago.

"Are you okay?" I asked when I didn't get a response.

Asher turned, surprising me when he wore an expansive grin rather than a frown. "Sorry, I'm fine. I was lost in thought. A memory came back to me of when Charlie and I played a prank on one of the guys in our barracks during training."

I loved seeing Asher smile like that. The way his eyes crinkled around the edges made my heart feel light enough that it could float away.

Motioning to the couch, I said, "I want to hear all about Charlie."

We sat, Asher's whole face lighting up as he told me about his best friend.

"He was everything I wasn't," Ash explained. "We complemented each other, getting along like brothers from the moment we met. He didn't have a family, so he became part of mine. My whole family loved him, especially my dad. It didn't hurt that he was a natural fisherman. If there's a seafaring gene, Charlie had it."

A lovely glow expanded through me as I listened, and I wished I could tuck myself close to Asher and hear his voice reverberate through his chest as he talked. But I knew even if I could lean on him, there wouldn't be a real chest behind the energy. As real as he seemed to me, I couldn't press my ear to his chest and hear him breathe or listen to his heartbeat.

Unaware of my inner thoughts, Asher continued talking. "Charlie was the bridge I needed between me and my dad.

Once I met Charlie, things started getting easier with Archie."

Even though I knew Asher's middle name, Archibald had also been his father's name. I'd never heard him call the man Archie before. It seemed like simply talking about Charlie made Asher friendlier toward his father.

"The mere fact that we were friends earned me points in Archie's eyes." Asher's chest puffed out slightly as he talked about it. "I'm glad he stuck around after I was gone. I'm sure that was a big help for my family."

I reached forward and Asher met me halfway, enveloping my hand in his. I squeezed tight. "He sounds like a great guy."

Asher hummed in agreement. "The best friend I've had … until you."

An electric current seemed to pass between our hands, and I slowly let go. It was all too much, too confusing, too impossible.

My discomfort didn't go unnoticed, and Asher's gaze dropped along with his hand, back to his lap.

Desperate to get us back to the happy place we'd been in moments before, I said, "Okay, you've got to tell me about this prank you two pulled."

Asher's lips pulled into a smirk, and his eyes danced with mischief. "Well, it all started with a hat."

4

A particularly loud seagull woke me early the next morning. From the sounds of cabinets opening and closing in the kitchen, Callie was already up and working on today's baked items. Saturdays tended to be our busiest day of the week, especially during the summer, so I knew she was probably making extra treats today.

I padded sleepily down the stairs and into the empty tearoom. The sound of wind and waves spilled through the windows we'd left cracked overnight to cool down the house. Bright blue water curled lazily toward the shoreline, finishing with more of a subdued splash rather than the normal cacophony. I took in the sight, the sun already shining brightly despite the early hour. My toes scrunched as the cold wood floors sucked the heat from my feet.

Starting a pot of tea, I brought it with me into the kitchen as it steeped. Delicious smells of sweet dough and cinnamon greeted me before I even stepped inside. After the chill I'd picked up in the tearoom, I didn't mind the heat spilling out from the oven, but I knew that wouldn't be the case later in the day when the thermometer ticked up into the eighties.

After waving sleepily at Callie and pouring her a cup of the tea I'd made, I curled into one of the chairs around the table situated in the small kitchen nook.

"No Ash this morning?" I asked and peered around the room.

Callie opened the oven door and removed a tray of golden brown cinnamon buns. "Nope. He wasn't around when I woke up." She set the finished tray on the stovetop to cool and replaced it with a batch of scones. Once she'd set a timer, she turned to me and studied me more closely. "You're up early."

"Seagull." I flapped a hand toward the window where the offending bird had been making all that racket.

Callie put a hand on her hip. "You sure that's all?"

I leaned back in the chair and brought my mug of tea up to my mouth, letting the steam swirl about my face in warm tendrils. Closing my eyes, I breathed in deep. "I think so, though I feel like I'm okay one moment and not okay the next."

"I hear you there." Callie leaned back on the counter and wiped her floury hands on her apron.

That made me sit forward. "Is everything okay with you and Owen?"

Had I been so focused on myself and my problems with Asher that I hadn't noticed Callie was struggling with something? I'd only been a sister for a couple of months at this point. How could I be failing already?

Callie's cheeks turned pink like they did whenever she blurted something out that she wished she hadn't said aloud.

She grabbed a kitchen towel off the counter and swatted it at me. "It's nothing. I was just commiserating."

I may have failed to see the signs before, but I was reading them loud and clear now. There was definitely something wrong. About to push her further on what was going on, I was interrupted when Lois appeared in the kitchen.

I let out a surprised yelp, and Callie jumped back, placing her hand over her heart.

"You'd think the two of you were new to this whole talking to spirits thing." Lois's tone was deadpan as was her expression.

"We're just not used to ghostly visitors this early," I said, taking another sip of my tea as I watched her with interest. Lois wasn't one to come hang at the tea shop, so if she was here, that meant there was something big happening.

"I don't think I'll ever get used to spirits appearing out of nowhere." Callie shook her head as she repositioned the kitchen towel on the oven door handle.

Lois snorted. "Fine. I won't tell you *all* the earth-shattering information I learned at the station this morning." She turned her ghostly back to us but peeked over one shoulder.

"It's pretty early for earth-shattering information," I said.

"The chief's been busy." Lois crossed her arms.

Callie pulled open the oven to check her scones. Seeing they were still going to need a while, she settled into the seat next to me at the small kitchen table, bringing her tea with her. "Okay, so what's the news?"

Lois settled in the last open seat and placed her translucent elbows on the table. "Things are not going well for the Rickster."

Sharing a quick look, Callie and I nodded. That wasn't exactly news, let alone earth-shattering.

"The chief and Gerard were up late last night doing research on this Captain Westover person. He was a multi-millionaire, and the Rickster stands to inherit his company." Lois's eyes lit up with the information. She was the only one of the local ghosts who could go inside the police station without having to be called using a moonstone, and she savored every morsel of power that gave her.

"He was telling the truth about the sail company they started together?" I asked.

Having been threaded into the explanation of their sailing trip around the world and climbing Mount Everest, I'd just assumed that the part about their shared business had been a lie as well.

Lois shrugged. "It seems like it. That's part of what took them so long to confirm. The Rickster, or Rick Rockefeller, isn't anywhere on the company paperwork. He doesn't technically own any part of the company, unless Captain Westover dies. Then he's the sole beneficiary of Cap's Sail Loft."

I took another long sip of my tea, hoping the caffeine might kick in and make all of this less confusing.

Lois kept talking. "The chief confirmed that the Rickster has been getting monthly payments from Captain's company. The Rickster's story is that he and Captain started the company together, but that he doesn't enjoy being involved in the day-to-day."

I snapped my fingers. "He mentioned that in his story at the crime scene."

Lois nodded. "But because he was so instrumental in the design of their most popular sail design, Captain has been sending him a monthly salary to pay for his part in the company."

"So that's how he always seems to have money." Callie slapped her leg. "I wondered what he'd done to keep paying his bills."

"But he also always seems broke," I countered. "If he's getting a monthly salary from a multimillion dollar company, why is he always scheming?"

Lois inclined her head. "That's part of the reason they worked out this deal, according to the Rickster. He's terrible with money, and always has been. Captain wanted to pay him for his help with the design, but he wasn't getting a *lot* each month since he wasn't involved in any of the running of the company. He said it was enough to get by, but not enough that he couldn't blow it on a 'pretty lady with a twinkle in her eye,'" Lois scoffed.

Asher appeared in the kitchen, making it feel a little cramped even though two of the people weren't actually taking up physical space.

"You find anything?" Lois asked him.

He scratched at the back of his neck. "He has the symbol for the company painted on the hull of his boat, like he told the chief." Asher raised his palms. "Though I'm not sure what that proves, exactly."

Lois turned to me and Callie. "The Rickster thought the chief could use the fact that he had the company symbol painted on the side of his houseboat as proof that he was a founder of Sail Lite."

"You'd think he'd be working to prove he doesn't have a connection with that company." Asher sighed.

"Right," I said, "because if the Rickster stood to gain that much from Captain's death, he had the best motive to kill him." My fingers curled around my mug. Even in the cozy, warm kitchen, the idea chilled me to the bone.

"And the means, since eyewitnesses saw him holding the knife." Callie checked her watch, standing up so she would be ready when her scones were.

Blinking, I said, "This is complicated."

"Very," Asher said, then he met Lois's gaze. "Speaking of complicated … did you ask her?" His eyes flicked to me.

"Ask me what?" I sat up.

Lois shook her head. "I hadn't gotten to that part yet."

"What?" I set down my mug of tea, wondering if I was going to need to brace myself for whatever request would follow all of that buildup.

Asher's eyebrows pulled together, making a crease form in between them. "It's Genny."

"Remember how scared she seemed when she saw those wet footprints the night of the murder?" Lois asked.

I nodded, though it had only been one minor detail amid many other shocking developments that evening.

"She's completely shut down," Asher said. "We can't get her to move from the cannery. She's just sitting in the corner, rocking back and forth, mumbling something about visions."

"That's awful," Callie said as she moved the cinnamon buns off the stovetop to make room for the tray of scones.

"We think it has to do with why her spirit is still here, about how she died." Lois held my gaze, then looked to

Asher as if he had the next line in a practiced scene from a play.

"And we want you to help us, Rosemary." Asher cleared his throat. "Help her."

Callie bent to pull the scones out of the oven, but she watched me out of the corner of her eye.

"The last time I even insinuated that she died of anything but natural causes, she'd thought I was rude and has treated me differently ever since." I cut the air with my hand. "Even if I tried, I doubt she would admit there was ever anyone who disliked her. Why don't you have Callie talk to her? She loves Callie."

Asher studied me for a moment before saying, "She specifically asked for you, Rosie."

That piece of information made my stiff shoulders soften. "She did?"

Lois snorted. "She did *not.*"

"Well, she mentioned that there was rosemary in one of her visions." Asher glared at Lois.

Lois studied the ceiling. "You may have a point because she said, 'Do you think that stands for the plant or that rude girl?'"

Callie giggled, hiding her grin behind the oven mitt.

I shifted my weight in discomfort. "I don't think this is a good idea. I'd be happy to research her life, but I think someone else should be the one to communicate with her instead of me." I crossed my arms.

Asher stepped forward. "Talk to her. That's all I ask." His blue eyes pleaded with me.

Holding my breath for a moment, I exhaled. "You know

I can't say no to that look." My lip twitched. "Fine. I'll talk to her."

"Too bad Asher's handsomeness can't work its magic on the Rickster's case like it just did on you, Rosie," Callie muttered. "That man's going to need all the help he can get if he doesn't want to spend the rest of his life behind bars."

5

The ghosts left Callie and me to open the tea shop, but my jumpiness stuck around. Between the murder in town, Genny's issues, and my worries about Asher leaving me too soon, the smallest things made me startle. A teacup being set down on the table too hard, the front door slamming shut, or someone laughing too loud made my heart race.

It was just after the Saturday lunch crowd when Riley rushed inside, clutching yellowed letters in his hand. His brown eyes shone with enthusiasm.

"What are you doing here?" I took a step back.

I'd just seen him yesterday. We weren't supposed to meet again for a week.

"Rosie, I need to talk to you." He placed a hand on each of my arms like he was about to pull me into a hug but held back. The letters crinkled as they crumpled against my arm.

My grumpy neighbor, Carl, was the only customer in the teahouse at the moment. He cleared his throat as he readjusted the newspaper he was reading. Carl was protective of me, having lost his own granddaughter to a swimming accident when she was ten. Callie and I were like his substitute granddaughters.

His eyes flicked to Riley's hands, gripping my arms. But I gave him a quick nod, showing him it was okay. Riley's grip was gentle. He was a lovely person, kind and always respectful. He was merely excited about something.

I narrowed my eyes, recognizing that brand of excitement. It was the same look Mom got whenever she'd found something big while researching. I was sure it was a look I'd adopted on more than one occasion while filling in Asher about something I'd learned in a case.

Riley had found something. Something big.

"What is it?" I asked, glancing over my shoulder.

The anxiety that had been rising up my neck in uncomfortable waves of heat subsided once I realized Asher wasn't in the room. If this really was a breakthrough in his case, at least I could stall and wait to tell him when I was ready.

Riley flapped the letters in front of me, pulling me toward a chair. "I reread that same letter from Catherine last night when I couldn't sleep. I had this weird feeling that I'd missed something. I thought she'd moved on to a different topic because I didn't see Charlie's or Asher's names anymore, but what I missed was that she mentioned someone named Lyle Hulquist."

I blinked. "Lyle?"

"He took over as manager of the company after Asher disappeared, once they were in Astoria." Riley's eyes flicked across my face, waiting for my reaction.

Lyle. I'd never heard his name mentioned during my research on Asher before. But something about the name sent a tingling dread down the length of my spine. Lyle. If he was the person who took over the company after Asher was gone, he had the best motive to kill him.

Dread flooded me, bringing an unsteady feeling with it. I felt like I was being swept under by a rogue wave, the current snatching me back under the water each time I tried to surface for air.

Needing some control over the situation, I poked holes in the theory. "Why would he kill Asher for the company *before* he went to fight in a war? Why didn't he just wait until Asher came back? *If* Asher came back."

"Because he *hated* Asher," Riley answered, dousing me again when he pulled out a second letter. "I'm sorry. I know I said I wouldn't do any research without you, but once I started digging, I couldn't stop." Riley unfolded the letter, eyes flashing with intrigue. "Catherine's next letter goes into more detail about Lyle. Apparently, he was the person who was just under Asher when he was in charge of the fishing company. He was going to step into Asher's role while he was away in the war.

"Hannah must've talked about how frustrated Lyle was taking a back seat to Asher in her last letter because Catherine responds by saying, *I am equally surprised to hear that Lyle is inept as a manager. I suppose I too assumed that he knew what he was doing, especially given how much he grumbled about how he could run the company better than Asher, who could barely keep his nose out of books. Well, I guess this proves he was all talk.*"

So Lyle had worked under Asher, and there was obvi-

ously a history of contention between the two. That gave
the man motive, for sure. And even though I didn't have any
proof that Lyle could've had the means or opportunity to
have done this, I felt it in my bones that this was the reason
Asher had died. Someone had killed him to get him out of
the way so they could take over his company.

The tea shop tilted around me. *Was this it?* If we'd had
any other suspects left, it might not have felt so final, but
Lyle was the only one.

Strong hands gripped my shoulders. "Rosemary, is
everything all right?" Carl's gravelly voice grounded me as
much as the weight of his hands pressing down on me. "You
don't look okay."

Footsteps scampered up behind me. "What's going on?"
Callie asked.

"Rosemary isn't feeling well," Carl said.

Riley just sat there. The letter still hung from his finger-
tips as he watched me from across the table. Callie moved
into my line of sight.

"Rosie," she said, snapping in front of my face. "Can
you hear me?"

I nodded.

"Come with me. Riley, I'm sorry. I think she just needs a
minute." She helped me stand and walked me into the other
part of the tea shop. "Carl, will you let me know if we get
any other customers?" she called over her shoulder as I
leaned into her, and we walked to the library.

The library was quiet and stuffy, with midday heat
streaming in through the large windows along the south-
western wall. My whole body relaxed when I saw that the
room was empty. Asher was nowhere to be found. He hadn't

heard anything Riley said. I slumped onto the worn leather couch.

"Was that it?" Callie asked, her voice strangled. "Did Riley find out who it was?" She knew a reaction this strong had to be in response to news about Asher.

Wringing my hands in my lap, I nodded, then quickly shook my head. "It could be. It's not definitive, but it seems pretty close. I got scared." The words croaked out of me.

Callie's face crumpled in on itself and she rushed toward me, pulling me into a tight hug. "I'm so sorry."

I wrapped my arms around her, hugging her just as fiercely, glad I had someone who understood. "I can't do it, Cal," I whispered into her hair. "I'm not strong enough to lose him."

Callie pulled back so she could meet my eyes. "You want me to tell Riley to leave?"

"I should be the one to do it." I got to my feet, my legs still a little unsteady.

Carl's gaze followed me protectively as I reentered the tearoom. Riley looked up, hope evident in his lifted brows.

"You doing okay?" he asked, his voice soft as he leaned toward me.

"I am." I settled in the chair across from him. "I'm so sorry. There's been a lot going on around here lately. A man was stabbed the other night, and hearing about murder again … I got overwhelmed."

Riley cut the air with his hand. "I shouldn't have come. I'm the one who should be sorry. Storming in here while you're working and bombarding you with information." His gaze dropped. "Just know I'm here if you need to talk."

I reached forward and grabbed his hands, squeezing

tight. "Riley, it's not your fault. You were excited. That's okay."

He lifted his chin. "Still, I promise to text next time instead of surprising you like that." He moved his hands so they were cupping mine. "I should get going." He glanced down at the letters on the table. "Do you want me to leave these here? It's only fair since I did some research without you."

"No," I blurted. My cheeks heated with embarrassment at my outburst. Much more quietly, I added, "No, thank you. You keep them." I eyed the letters like they might be poisonous snakes instead of yellowed pieces of paper.

They might as well have been snakes, with how dangerous they felt to me. Having them around here was the last thing I wanted.

Riley folded up the letters and nodded. He tapped them to his forehead in a salute. "Okay, I hope the rest of your day goes better, Rosie."

I waved, clasping my hands together after so they wouldn't shake. I turned around, ready to busy myself with work. Carl stood just behind me. I let out a small yelp of surprise.

He fixed me with his signature scowl. I expected him to ask me what was really going on. Instead, he stepped forward and pulled me into the tightest hug I'd been on the receiving end of in a while. I sank into him. His shirt smelled of spicy cologne and wood shavings, even though I was sure he hadn't been around any construction projects since he helped me rebuild my tea shed in the backyard last summer. I let my arms wrap around him and closed my eyes.

"Hang in there, little one," he muttered into my ear. "I'm not sure what you're going through, but it always gets easier. I promise. Time may not heal all wounds, but it definitely takes the sting away."

My face crumpled, every part of me wanting to break into sobs. But I pulled in a deep breath through my nose. "Thank you."

The bell on the front door of the tea shop jingled, ending our moment. I smiled once more at Carl before turning to greet my next customer.

————

I WAS STACKING the dirty dishes into the dishwasher after we closed that afternoon when Asher appeared in the tearoom. The way his face brightened the moment he saw me felt like a kick to the gut.

He glanced around the empty room at the last few dirty dishes sitting on tables. "Here, let me help." He gathered the rest of the teacups and brought them over to me, sliding them on the bar.

For some reason, it made me want to cry. "Thanks," I croaked out, clearing my throat self-consciously as I pretended that hadn't happened to my voice.

He leaned his forearms on the tea bar, studying me. It was just the two of us in the house. Callie had left a little before closing to meet Owen for a hike before dinner.

"What's going on in that head of yours?" Asher asked. One side of his mouth tipped up into a half smile, but his blue eyes held me tight, showing me he was taking my odd mood seriously.

I pushed you to get the closure you need to leave, and now I'm not sure I can say goodbye. The thought stayed locked tight inside my brain.

Instead, I said, "It's just been a weird day." I looked down, fiddling with the dishwasher longer than I needed to in order to let my emotions pass. When I stood, however, they all came rushing back to me.

Asher's dark hair fell forward onto his forehead. Intelligent blue eyes blinked back at me. It was amazing how someone who didn't even have a physical body could emanate so much warmth, but Asher was my home.

I should've asked him about Lyle right away, to figure out if there was anything to the clue Riley had uncovered. But I couldn't.

"I was thinking of making a new blend," I said, shutting the dishwasher and moving around the tea bar, grabbing a notepad and pen on my way past. "I thought I could make it in honor of you."

His smile slid over to the other side of his mouth. "Asher tea?" He pivoted as his eyes followed me.

I slipped onto a stool. "I mean, obviously we would call it something different, like the Sunset blend. But I want to make one that reminds me of you, always."

His smile fell. Sadness darkening his normally bright eyes, as if he knew why I was feeling nostalgic. "Rosie." His voice cracked around my name. "It's going to be okay. You know that, right?" He took a step toward me.

I waved my hands. "I know. It'll be fine. I mean, except that it won't. I won't." Tears crowded my eyes, and the memory of the moment with Riley earlier fell over me again.

Ash closed the space in between us and wrapped me into a hug. It was completely different from Carl's hug earlier today. While I felt safe in both, Carl's hug felt like he was trying to squeeze the sadness out of me. Asher's hugs filled me with love, like he would give me every last bit of his energy if he could.

He lifted me off the stool, waiting until my feet settled on the floor before tucking me back under his chin and surrounding me with his arms. I wished he had a smell that I could breathe in, that I could remember forever. I supposed that was where the idea of a tea came from. It was a scent I could hold on to when I could no longer hold on to him.

"I'm sorry if you had a rough day," he whispered in my ear.

My heart fluttered, along with my eyelids.

After a moment, he stepped back, slightly dimmer than he had been before. That kind of pressure took a lot out of him.

"So, Sunset tea?" He slid onto the seat next to me.

I swallowed, regaining my composure as I took my seat again. I showed him I was ready with the pen.

He glanced up at the ceiling in thought. "I love cinnamon," he said. "So that has to be part of the blend."

A warmth expanded through my chest. I imagined him smelling of the spice and I couldn't help but relax.

"It's gotta be a black tea," he said seriously.

"Full of caffeine because you haven't slept in a century?" I guessed.

His lips arched into a grin. "I was thinking because I

have a dark and twisty soul, but I like your reasoning better."

"Ash, your soul is the opposite of dark," I said. "It's the lightest, most joyful soul I've ever experienced in my life."

His eyes held mine for a second before he nodded. We added a few other small things to the list, and after a moment he asked, "Ready to talk about what's really going on?"

My gaze fell and shook my head. "Any news in town?"

Ash sighed. "Being locked up has the Rickster acting even more odd than usual."

The Rickster.

A solution to my problem presented itself so perfectly in front of me. We needed to help the Rickster by finding out who killed his friend and left him to take the blame. It wouldn't be easy, and would likely take all of my mental energy, which meant I would need to put a pin in working on Asher's mystery while I focused on the killer on the loose. It also meant Asher and I could work on one more investigation together.

Perking up at the realization, I said, "I think we should help him."

Asher's eyebrows jumped up.

"Don't you?" I asked, leaning forward, excitement pulsing through my body. "I mean, the poor guy is the sole suspect. You and Lois both said it's not looking good for him. It could be fun." The words *one last mystery* hung on the tip of my tongue. I didn't want Asher to know how close we were to solving his murder, though I thought for sure he could feel it.

After contemplating the idea for a moment, Asher said, "As long as you help Genny too. I'm in."

Sticking my hand out, I waited until he took mine. We shook on it.

6

I lost myself in testing out different trials of my Asher-inspired Sunset tea for the rest of the evening. I stayed up late into the night after Callie came home, half because of all the black tea I'd consumed through my taste testing and half because I couldn't shut off my mind.

Luckily, Callie and I had prearranged to close the tea shop the next day so we could spend Sunday in the cove with Jolene and Beck. We were finally going to try out their beloved stand-up paddleboarding.

But I'd also made a promise to Asher to help Genny, so I wanted to go talk to her before we headed into town. Callie volunteered to join me, which settled my nerves at least a little. If things went sideways, Callie could always step in with Genny.

We drove out to the cannery, where Genny was hiding. Anxiety clawed at my stomach as I drove, and my fingers gripped the steering wheel even tighter than normal as I crested the hill next to the treacherous Desperation Cliff.

Callie sat silently next to me. Either she knew me too

well to lie to me and tell me it was all going to be okay, or she was feeling just as anxious about the impending conversation.

Once we parked, we hurried into the cannery, finding the group of ghosts waiting for us on the second floor, where we usually met when we all gathered here. Genny sat in the corner, her knees pulled up tight to her chest, arms wrapped around them like she was worried someone was going to come grab her at any second.

Seeing the look on the ghost's face, the terror clear in her wide eyes and stiff posture, made me scold myself for not coming out sooner. The poor thing was in a legitimate state. I'd never seen her like this before.

The spirit in front of me was in distress.

My gaze flicked to Asher, and he furrowed his brow for a second, silently telling me not to blame myself, as he knew I had been.

Kneeling next to her about a yard away—I wasn't sure if she would flee if I got too close—I said, "Genny, it's Rosemary." She seemed so different, so out of it, I wasn't sure if she would even recognize that I was there. "And Callie too," I mentioned as my sister knelt next to me. "We're here to help."

Genny's rocking stopped. Her features softened, then crumpled again, and I thought she might cry. "I know who you are. I still have eyes, you know," she scoffed.

Callie and I shared a quick smirk. She was still Genny.

Scooting a little closer, I sat and crossed my legs in front of me. "Can you tell me about the visions, Genny?" I asked softly.

Her wrinkled fingers curled into tight fists, but then they

relaxed. "I've always been clairvoyant. Well, when I was alive." She swallowed and looked up at me, her light blue eyes meeting mine. "I had a knack for seeing snippets of things before they would happen."

I blinked in surprise. I'd recently met an herbal witch who was highly clairvoyant, so I didn't doubt those people existed—heck, I could communicate with ghosts, so nothing seemed out of the realm of believability now—but I had never pictured someone like Genny as a part of that group. I nodded for her to continue.

"I had a vision of my dad falling off our roof when I was about six, so I warned him not to go up there. He didn't listen to me and fell, broke his leg in two places." She tsked. "Luckily, he healed, and he—and the rest of my family—took me seriously after that." Her spine straightened with pride as she said, "I think I did a lot of good throughout my life." Her gaze sharpened, and she looked squarely into my eyes. "As I've said before, everyone loved me."

I pressed my lips together to hold in my reaction. What was that Shakespeare line: "The lady doth protest too much, methinks"? It felt too fitting, considering the ferocity and fervor Genny used when she made her claim.

Her transparent fingers trembled, and she laced them together to stop them from shaking. "Mostly, I would see the visions only once. I would get a glimpse and they would be gone, whether the people I told heeded them or not. It was like a flash." Her nostrils flared. "Except for one. Well, one grouping of visions."

Callie and I leaned closer. Everyone was silent as we listened. The sound of the waves crashing at the beach below the cliffs was the only soundtrack other than Genny's soft voice.

"In my early twenties, I started to see a succession of four visions. One after another. They flashed into my mind just as all of the others had. But instead of being single snapshots, these four were always grouped together. I saw them my whole life, until the day I died."

In bed, in her sleep, I filled in the bit I was sure she was thinking but didn't say.

"And those visions never appeared in your daily life?" I asked.

She shook her head but stopped. "Not until now."

My throat felt dry.

"The first of the four visions was a wet patch on a wooden boardwalk, footprints leading away from the water into the night."

Goose bumps tingled over my bare arms. The warm summer day suddenly felt icy cold. That was why she'd freaked out so intensely at the sight of the wet footprints on the night Captain was murdered.

"The second is a sprig of rosemary. The third is a letter with a green wax seal and a bend in the right corner. And the fourth is—" Genny closed her eyes tight.

"What is it?" Callie asked, reaching a hand out instinctively before she remembered she couldn't touch Genny, and she pulled her hand back.

Tears welled in the older woman's eyes, spilling over onto her cheeks. "A man being murdered."

I'm not sure if I gasped, or if we all did, but surprise hung heavy in the dusty air of the concrete cannery.

"Had you ever seen anything like that before in your visions?" I asked carefully.

Genny shook her head vigorously. "No, it was all small things, like a friend walking out of the library and running into someone who would later become their spouse. Or my mom burning her hands on the oven because her oven mitt slipped. I would tell her to be extra careful when she was making a pie that day, or recommend that my friend visit the library that week, etcetera." Genny circled her hands in front of her. "It was never murder … until that one." She shivered. "And those visions have been on repeat almost my whole life."

Ideas and revelations began lining up in my mind. I tempered what I said next, knowing Genny and I had a history of misunderstandings. "Genny, this could be your unfinished business."

Her eyes flashed up to mine, as if to tell me to watch what I said next.

I held up a hand. "Hear me out. You said you died in your sleep, but your spirit is still here because it has something it still needs to do. What if you are the only one who can stop this murder from occurring?"

She didn't nod, but she didn't frown either. In fact, her face softened like that was the only thing I'd ever said that made sense to her.

Encouraged, I kept talking. "What if the visions repeated your whole life because this is something so important it couldn't go unnoticed?" I sucked in a quick inhale. If this was connected to the wet footprints, it could have to do with Captain Westover's murder. "Maybe you're here to stop another murder from happening. Can you tell us about the murder in your last vision?"

As we'd been talking, Genny's posture had loosened; her legs had scooted away from her body ever so slightly. She wasn't so tightly wound.

But at my question about the murder, she closed back up, hugging her legs tight. "I can't." She squeezed her eyes shut as she shook her head. "I can't talk about it."

"Okay," I said softly. "You said it was a man. Was he young or old?" I asked, trying a different tactic.

"No!" she screamed. She scooted away from me like I'd burned her. "I can't. I don't want to."

Surprise made me lift my hands up in a calming gesture. "Okay, you don't need to." I glanced around the room, catching everyone else's serious stares. "But, Genny, if I'm the rosemary in your second vision, which I'd be flattered to think I am, I think it means that I can help you with this."

She peeled open her eyes and glared at me, expecting me to ask her to describe the murder again.

I spoke slowly, carefully. "You tell me when you're ready to talk. Okay?"

She nodded.

"In the meantime, I need you to keep an eye out for any sprigs of rosemary that you encounter, just in case it's another clue, and it's not actually about me."

Genny sat up straighter. It would probably make her very happy to discover I wasn't part of her visions. "I will," she said.

Seeing her body loosen up once more, I tried something I knew might be risky. "I think it's important for you to go about your normal routines, Genny. As much as I understand the instinct to hide away, I have a feeling that you'll get more answers if you go about your days normally."

Looking around at the other ghosts, the spirits she usually spent her time with, Genny said, "All right." Slowly, she stood.

Callie and I followed suit. We both gave her beaming, encouraging smiles.

"You're very brave, Genny," Callie said.

I nodded in agreement.

The other ghosts chimed in with similar sentiments. "We'll stay by your side, Genny," they said. "We'll help you figure this out."

She pulled in a deep breath even though she didn't have any lungs. It was an emotional reset more than anything now. Squaring her shoulders, she said, "If I stop this murder from taking place, maybe I'll get to move on, finally." The way her voice lightened dreamily at the phrase "move on" made me glance over at Asher.

Genny had only been stuck here as a ghost for less than a decade. Asher had already exceeded a century since his death.

When I'd first met him, it had been all he'd wanted: to be at peace. It was what most ghosts I'd met wanted. And as final, and quick, as the moving-on process was, each spirit I'd witnessed pass on seemed completely and utterly at peace. There was never a hint of regret in them as they left.

That was what I wanted for Asher. He deserved that all-encompassing peace. But I could still feel doubt in him, or maybe that was my inability to let him go that caused him so much apprehension about moving on.

"Thank you," Genny said, smiling at me for the first

time in a while. "Maybe you aren't so bad after all, Rosemary."

I chuckled. "I'll take that as a compliment."

Callie checked her watch. "We should get going if we want to meet Jolene on time."

We waved goodbye to everyone and headed to the car. Thoughts of Genny's connection to this murder investigation made me realize I was meant to get involved in this. It was fate. If Genny had started seeing those visions in her twenties, this murder investigation was at least sixty years in the making.

As my fingers closed over the car door handle, I let go of the guilt that had cropped up during my talk with Genny. Maybe putting off Asher's mystery for a little longer was just what the universe intended for me to do.

7

―――――――

"Is it weird to admit that I'm looking forward to paddleboarding?" Callie asked as we piled back into my car in the cannery parking lot.

I shot a wary glance over at her. "Yes. It is weird. Please don't do this to me. I don't think I could handle it if you became obsessed with this too," I grumbled.

Callie snorted out a laugh. "I'm not excited because of the paddleboarding, per se. I'm excited that we'll finally get Jo off our backs about trying it."

Chuckling, I pulled out of the cannery parking lot and drove toward town. "That makes more sense."

The sun was already pulsing heat down on the small coastal town. It hung in the sky, covering everything it touched with glittering light and warmth. We had swimsuits on underneath shorts and tank tops, hoping we wouldn't fall into the water, but prepared just in case.

"I guess I'm excited too. Focusing on not falling into the water will be a good way to take my mind off everything else," I said as I rounded a bend in the road.

I felt Callie's worried gaze on me. "Did you talk to Asher about Lyle last night?" she asked.

I'd been too immersed in tea blending and scratching down recipe notes to get into it last night when Callie got home.

Shaking my head, I said, "I ended up suggesting we help figure out how to get the Rickster out of the trouble he's in." As the cove came into view, I squeezed the steering wheel tighter. "I'm a coward, and I'm stalling."

Callie reached over and squeezed my shoulder. "You're not a coward. You're dealing with a lot of scary emotions. I understand."

I placed my hand over hers for a moment before letting it drop into my lap. "Thanks for understanding. I can't believe how reckless I've been with my time with him."

There were so many moments over the last two years that I thought I was about to lose him, but there was something different about this time. This felt more serious, more final, which scared me even more.

"Don't feel guilty." Callie's tone bordered on commanding. "Give yourself this last mystery together. Journal about your time together, about what you love about him. Be selfish so that you can let him go when you need to."

Pressing my lips into a hard line, I contemplated what she was saying.

"You're right." I parked in front of Jolene's tea shop. "Thank you. I just have to figure out how to convince Riley to put our research on pause. He reminds me of Mom when she has a lead. I don't think he wants to stop. He's like a—" I stopped short, trying to think of an analogy other than a dog with a bone.

"A Jolene with a hobby?" Callie suggested, gesturing out the windshield to our friend waving wildly at us, a large paddleboard propped up next to her.

I nodded. "Yeah, like that."

We got out of the car and prepared for our lesson. My excitement skyrocketed as I noticed Asher standing nearby. I'd invited him but wasn't sure if he would come, not being able to take part in the activity. He held up a hand in a wave as Callie and I approached Jolene.

"I can't believe you're finally going to try this." Jolene's whole body tensed with excitement.

Beck grinned at her enthusiasm. He turned and moved toward a large grouping of paddles and boards.

My eyes flicked over the equipment, counting twice before I turned back to Jolene. "Wait. I thought you only had two of these." I pointed at the large floating devices.

Jolene scrunched her nose guiltily. "We may have bought a few more," she admitted sheepishly but put a hand up like a stop sign. "Not *just* for you and Callie to try. There's no pressure for you to continue after today."

"Sure there isn't," Callie mumbled under her breath to me.

I coughed to cover up a laugh.

"We're actually looking into setting up a rental business on the side," Beck explained, walking forward and handing over a paddle to each of us. "I could run it while Jolene runs the tea shop."

I studied the paddle, gripping the end and practicing a stroke. "That sounds fun!" I glanced over at Jolene.

My friend seemed so alive, so happy. It reminded me of how much she had gone through to get where she was today.

She'd dated a lot of terrible partners before she found Beck. She'd been so worried that she was cursed to be cheated on in every relationship that she even tried out a nickname so she could get space between her real name, the title of the famous Dolly Parton song. But ever since she'd met Beck, she'd gone back to using Jolene, no longer feeling like it was cursed.

I tried to apply that lens to my life. Things seemed bad now, but I would be okay in the long run. I had to be. Callie was right. This was the time to savor every moment with Asher. Nothing in my life had been normal up to this point, so why would my first love be any different?

"Well, we're happy to be your test subjects," Callie said, grabbing a paddle of her own.

Minutes later, we were perched at the water's edge, life jackets on, gripping our paddles. I crawled unsteadily onto my board, Jolene directing me with her words from the shore.

"That's it. Start on your knees. You can wait until you get your balance there and then stand up." Her tone was calm.

Callie paddled out slightly in front of me. She wore a huge grin. "Okay, this is kind of fun," she admitted as she turned back toward Jolene.

"Told you," Jo called from the shore.

Callie shot forward, her paddling skills already cemented. She took a tentative moment to steady herself as she got to her feet. She wobbled for a second but got her balance. Paddling around to face the shore, she said, "I did it!"

Jolene cheered, and I clapped awkwardly while still

gripping my paddle. I followed Callie. She made it look easy, so after a few more strokes, I placed the paddle on the board like she'd done and shakily got to my feet. I was about to let out a similar celebration when the board wobbled to the right, and my body overcorrected to the left.

I could feel myself going over, but something stopped me, righting me back onto the board.

"Whoa, there," Asher said, his hands steadying me. He "stood" on the board in front of me, smiling as he caught me.

Jolene gasped in surprise. "I could've sworn you were going in, Rosie." She beamed as she got on her own board and paddled over to us with Beck.

"Thanks," I whispered to Asher, who gave me a sly wink. "I'm all good," I said, louder so my friends could hear.

Once I was up, I got the hang of it, paddling around and laughing. Asher stayed with me on my board, and I stayed far enough from the others that he and I could chat and no one noticed when he caught me again the next two times I wobbled. I paddled out as far as the marina. The Rickster's blue houseboat, floating peacefully at the dock, reminded me that today wasn't only fun and games. I needed to stop by and talk to him about the case after we were done here.

I was heading back to shore, the late-morning sun becoming a little too hot, when my paddle struck something at the bottom of the cove. It had scraped against a few rocks in shallower sections of the cove already, but this time I heard a metallic *clink*. Asher's eyes cut over to mine before he leaned over, peering into the water. We floated over that spot, waiting for the murky water to clear, but we couldn't see anything underneath.

Asher held up a finger. "I'm going to check it out," he said.

"The saltwater will make you go all fuzzy," I warned him.

We'd found that the old wives' tale about throwing salt over your shoulder might've had some merit to it after all. Large quantities of salt made spirits distorted and unable to use energy for a time after.

"I'll risk it," he said decisively. "I'm too curious."

Just as he was about to go into the water, the sand and silt finally cleared enough, and I caught a glint of metal.

"Is that an air tank?" I asked.

"Like divers use?" Asher squinted at the water.

I nodded. "I think so."

While Asher was from the early nineteen hundreds, he was an avid reader and kept up on modern advances in technology and science through his daily newspaper perusals. If he hadn't learned about diving from newspapers, I was sure he'd seen them around the marina. Some of the larger fishing boats required divers to clean the parts of their hulls that weren't accessible above the water.

I shaded my eyes as I looked behind me. We were about halfway between the Rickster's houseboat and the shore.

"And it looks new," I said.

"Very new." Asher's lips flashed with a smile.

Diving equipment fit with the wet footprints leading away from the boardwalk, and the Rickster's claim that he hadn't seen the killer on the dock. If the killer had a diving suit, they could've stabbed Captain and then escaped under the water, using the cover of darkness to slink off into the night while everyone else was focused on the murder scene at the dock. And depending on how long they had to wait underwater, the killer might've stashed an extra tank just in case.

"I'll add this to the list of things I need to let the chief know," I said, noticing that Callie, Jolene, and Beck were waving me in. I followed, glancing back a few more times so I could describe the location of the air tank correctly to the chief.

"That was a lot of fun!" Callie stepped off her board like a professional.

"See?" Jolene stretched her arms out wide. "I told you."

I flailed around in the shallow water a little, trying to find my footing in the rocky cove. I was glad to be back on land.

Beck took care of our boards, stacking them vertically under the porch of Jolene's shop as Callie and Jolene chatted.

"Anyone up for lunch?" Callie asked, looking over at the Marina Mug.

My stomach rumbled in reply. Macaroni and cheese sounded great right now. We waited for Beck to lock up the boards and then walked over. Comfort food was just what I needed.

While we ate, Beck filled us in on his whole paddleboard rental plan. It made sense. The man worked remotely and could complete his work whenever he had time during the day. Running rentals during peak hours during the summer would only increase their cash flow and add a fun activity for locals to try.

Walking out of the Marina Mug after lunch, we were all smiles. But mine dropped into a frown as I noticed a grouping of police officers congregating outside the police station across the street. Officers Gerard, Kennedy, and Fischer stood there, all three of their brows furrowed with concern. Their postures mirrored one another as well, each crossing their arms stiffly in front of themselves.

Even more interesting, the ghost of former Police Chief Butler was outside with them, pacing and muttering to himself in an even more disgruntled way than normal.

Callie and I glanced at each other.

"Thanks for the lesson today," I said to Jolene and Beck.

"You're welcome … any time." Jolene waved.

Beck wrapped an arm around her shoulders and kissed her forehead as they headed back toward Jolene's shop. The sight of it made my heart feel a little less broken, while causing other areas to crack.

Callie must've figured out what I was thinking because she tucked her arm through mine, and we walked over to talk to the police officers. Fischer turned and caught sight of Callie as we approached. His frown softened, and a smile pulled over his face. I let go of her arm, smiling as Owen wrapped Callie into a hug.

My mind whirred as I thought through her awkwardness yesterday. My first worry had been that there was something wrong with her relationship, but they seemed to be fine. Maybe everything really was okay.

"I saw you out there paddling," he said, tipping his chin toward the cove. "You looked like a pro."

Callie's cheeks were pink from the sun. "It was really fun. I'll have to get you out there sometime." She peered around him at the station and the other officers. "What's going on here?"

Owen's expression tightened back to its upset state. "The Rickster's driving us all mad. We needed a break."

"He's still in there?" I asked, counting the days since Captain's murder in my head. I thought I remembered the chief saying something about how they could only hold suspects for a couple days without charging them with a crime. "Did the chief charge him?"

Gerard scoffed, "Not yet, and now he's out of town."

"Where'd he go?" Callie asked.

"Up to Astoria to look into Captain's business," Gerard said.

"Did he find anything?" I asked, wondering if he'd learned new information that made him doubt the Rickster enough not to charge him.

"Nothing new," Owen said. "It's the time of death that's giving the chief pause. That's the only thing on the Rickster's side at the moment. The chief feels like there's enough doubt that he wants to do more investigating."

"What about the time of death is giving him pause?" I asked. We'd basically been there when it had happened.

"The time between when everyone saw the Rickster leaving the Geoduck and when Chance saw him pull the knife out of Captain's stomach isn't enough for a man to bleed out. The chief thinks Captain had to have been stabbed at least five minutes before the Rickster left the Geoduck," Gerard explained to us. The flat tone of her voice told me she had her doubts.

"But if the chief hasn't charged the Rickster, why doesn't he just let him leave?" Callie asked, adding, "If he's getting on everyone's nerves, that seems like the smart thing to do."

Snorting, Owen said, "Yeah, he tried that. Let Rick go two days ago before he left for Astoria, but Rick came back the next morning, ranting about assassination attempts. He says the jail cell is the only place he feels safe."

I sent a worried frown over to Callie.

"Someone tried to kill him?" I asked.

Kennedy stepped forward at that moment. "It was probably a seagull dropping a clam too close to his head. It's all bravado."

"Why would he lie?" Callie asked, then seemed to regret her question as it all clicked.

"Because if he can distract us by thinking he's the next victim, then we won't look into him as the obvious suspect," Owen explained.

"Which he is," Gerard said.

"Or he can't admit what he's done yet, and his guilty conscience wants to be locked up," Kennedy said with a shrug.

We stood there awkwardly for a moment while we digested that notion.

"Can you take a walk?" Callie asked Owen, breaking the silence. The tightness to her voice made it sound like she needed to discuss something important with him.

Owen flinched for a quick moment but checked with Gerard, who waved him off.

Callie started walking but looked over her shoulder. "Rosemary, Owen can give me a ride home later if you want to go back to the tea shop."

I nodded, chewing on my lip as they left. The good feelings I'd gotten when we'd first arrived, vanished. Maybe there was something wrong with Callie and Owen.

Once they were out of earshot, I turned to Gerard and Kennedy. "Hey, I found something in the water, and since the chief's gone, I figured you two should know."

Their eyes widened with interest as I talked.

"This is great," Kennedy said, rubbing his hands together. "I love any chance I get to use the department boat."

Gerard snorted. "'Boat' is generous. It's a dingy." She turned to me. "Thank you, Rosemary. This is good information."

"Anytime." I smiled. But before they walked away, I said, "Since I told you that, is there any way you can do me a favor?"

They stared at me.

"I'd like to talk to the Rickster." I checked with Gerard, knowing she would be in charge in the chief's absence. "If that's okay?"

The police officer motioned for me to follow her inside. If I was going to get to the bottom of what happened to the Rickster's friend, I needed to go right to the source. I just wished my source was a little more reliable.

8

G erard walked me back to the single jail cell in the Pebble Cove Police Department building. I glanced down the hallway toward the chief's office. I wasn't sure how Raymond would feel about me talking to a man he'd brought in for questioning about a murder, so I was glad he was out of town.

There *was* still a police chief with me, however. Chief Butler's ghost followed me down the hall after Officer Gerard, complaining as per usual.

"I don't know who this guy thinks he is, but he can't stay here. This is my home." The ghostly police chief harrumphed as he crossed his arms in front of his chest.

Making sure Gerard wasn't looking my way, I chanced a glance over at the spirit. I hoped my unimpressed, flat expression showed him he had no leg to stand on when it came to deciding what was best for this department. He'd run a corrupt police force and, because of that, had almost gotten away with the murder of his own wife.

Gerard led me through a door, the scent of metal and

salty sea air prevalent. An open window in the concrete room answered the question about the seawater smell, and the metal bars of the jail cell answered for the other scent. Inside the cell, on a bench that I guessed also doubled as a bed, if need be, sat the Rickster. He wasn't hunched over forlornly or crumpled in defeat. His feet were kicked up. A houseboat magazine was open in his hands. He looked more like he was on vacation than in jail.

"You've got company, Rick." Gerard knocked a fist against the metal bars. "Unless, that is, you're finally ready to tell me the truth," she said hopefully.

The Rickster let out a dry laugh, not even glancing up from his magazine.

Gerard shrugged and motioned me forward.

I stepped around her, closing in on the metal bars as the Rickster finally made eye contact. He folded up the magazine and said, "Ah," as if he'd been expecting me. "Don't tell me." He tilted his head to one side. "You've been thinking about it for a few months, and you'd finally like to ask me out after our first two dates." He flashed me a toothy grin that may or may not have been dentures.

Gerard cringed, and I coughed in surprise.

"*Speed dating* dates," I quickly clarified, my gaze skirting nervously over to Gerard. "And we only had two because Fischer paid him so he could have a second date with Callie," I clarified.

I wasn't sure who I was trying to convince, because Gerard rolled her shoulders back in a stretch like she couldn't care less. "My office is right down the hall. Just holler if you need anything."

Chief Butler's ghost floated right through the metal

bars, settling next to the Rickster. "I hope you're here to get him to confess so we can charge him and send him upstate."

"I'll get right on that," I mumbled at the ornery ghost.

The Rickster's wild, white eyebrows lifted with interest. "Where should we get started, then?" he asked, having heard me and assumed I was talking to him, not the ghost sitting next to him.

I guess that worked as well as any segue into the conversation he and I needed to have.

"If you didn't kill Captain Westover, who might've wanted him dead?" I asked, pulling up a folding chair from the corner of the room and placing it on the other side of the metal bars.

"I can't think of a soul." The Rickster shrugged. There was a momentary sadness to his posture, but he brightened as he continued to talk about his friend. "The man was a saint. The best of the best. He was like all the greatest characters in literature rolled into one man. He was funny, kind, adventurous, thoughtful, moral, and a heck of a fighter." At this, the Rickster turned to his right and shadowboxed for a few seconds, like I wouldn't have known what he meant without a demonstration.

Unbeknownst to him, he had turned toward Chief Butler's ghost and was punching him right in the chest with each jab.

The spirit sputtered out an indignant string of curses as he moved out of the way. The Rickster stopped, taking a moment to study his knuckles which were most likely tingling with the icy sensation that came upon contact with a spirit. He dropped his hands down by his sides.

"All the greatest characters in literature rolled into one?" I repeated his line.

That was some praise. And while the Rickster wasn't a monthly staple at our Tea by the Sea book club, I knew the man had at least read *some* of the classics. He'd named his pet duck Atticus.

The Rickster nodded solemnly. "I hadn't seen the man in about a year, so it's possible he could've turned into a complete monster in that time." He blinked. "Possible, but not probable. If you want to know about Cap's day-to-day stuff, his assistant, Matt, is the one to ask. He's always who I talked to when I wanted to get in touch with the old guy."

"At the sail loft?" I asked, squinting one eye as I made sure I got the name correct.

"In Astoria. Our sails were the best in the West." He puffed out his chest proudly, even though it sounded like he had little to do with the running of the company.

Astoria. The fact that the chief was there investigating as we spoke wasn't the only reason my ears perked up at the mention of the city on the border between Oregon and Washington. Other than being the setting of some of the iconic shots from the eighties' movie, *The Goonies*, and the house from *Kindergarten Cop* in the nineties, the city sat on the Columbia River just before it met up with the Pacific Ocean. It was a boating paradise for fishing and sailing alike. And it just so happened to be the place where Asher's family business had moved after World War I, and where it had gone under about a decade later.

"Clemenson questioned this Matt guy?" I asked.

The Rickster dipped his head. "Before he even left for Astoria. He got him on the phone. I overheard Raymond telling Gerard that the kid has an alibi. He takes his mom to bingo every Thursday evening at the local community center. Plus, he absolutely adored Cap."

"It sounds like everyone did," I observed.

"Not everyone, apparently." The Rickster clicked his tongue.

Touché.

My attention returned to the man in the cell. "Why are you still in here? Really." I leveled him with a no-nonsense stare.

He opened both his palms. "The person who killed Captain is after me. I went home last night and there was an assassination attempt. I won't be a sitting duck in my house-boat for them to come and kill. If they want me, they'll have to figure out a way in here."

I cocked my head. "I mean, I got in here. Gerard's not even watching us."

He scoffed. "You're not here to kill me." But his mustache twitched, and he narrowed his eyes at me all the same.

The Rickster looked worried enough that I said, "Of course I'm not here to kill you. I want to help you."

He combed his fingers through his white mustache. "Thank you." After that moment of gratefulness, the man's posture tensed again. "But if you really want to help me, you'd catch this killer."

Luckily for him, that was exactly what I intended to do.

Pulling in a deep, steadying breath, I said, "Okay, tell me all about the assassination attempt."

The Rickster's beady, different-colored eyes flicked around the room. He swiped his hands in front of him to set the scene. "I went back home last night. Got there around eleven. Trickster and Atticus were out of food, so I tended to them right away," he said, knowing I'd already met his pets —a raccoon and duck—both of whom he was, strictly speaking, not supposed to have as pets. "But while I was mashing up a fresh batch of food, someone triggered my trip wire."

"How do you know?" I asked.

He flared his nostrils like he couldn't believe I would ask such a silly question. "Because I have it set to play duck quacking sounds when someone bumps it. That way, they just think it's Atticus quacking." He pinched at his chin with his index finger and thumb. "Though, now that you mention it, that's probably counterintuitive, given that I don't want people to know I have a duck living on my houseboat."

I held in a chuckle. The Rickster was a mess.

"Anyway"—the Rickster blinked, hopefully getting back to the story—"I waited and listened. Just about a minute later, someone tried to open my sliding door, but good thing I'd locked it behind me."

"Did you go to the door?" I asked, leaning forward. "Did you see who it was?"

"No," he said with a snort. "I hid. It was the stabber. I'm sure of it." His eyes were wild.

"Well, you're not sure, because you didn't see the person in either instance," I pointed out, knowing my criticism would go unheeded.

"Whatever." The Rickster crossed his arms. "Believe me or don't. But if you want to know who stabbed my friend, watch my boat tonight. I bet the killer will be back. They seemed like the kind to try again." The Rickster pushed up the sleeves on his button-up shirt. "Mostly given that they tried my slider twice. I'd at least expect them to try to kill me twice." He nodded, happy with his logic.

I pinched the bridge of my nose. "I'm not staking out your houseboat."

He sighed, like he'd expected as much. "Could you at least go inside and feed Trickster and Atticus?" The Rickster held up an index finger.

My jaw jutted back. "I don't want to go inside. What if the killer mistakes me for you?"

"Ah, so you admit that there's someone trying to kill me. Ha ha!" He pointed at me, as if he'd caught me in a trap. After I stood, placing my hand on my hip, he said, "Their food is in containers in the fridge."

"And how am I supposed to get inside?" I asked, expecting there to be a hidden door I had to access from the underside of the boat or something equally difficult.

The Rickster fished around in his pocket and produced a key. "Here."

I almost wanted to laugh. That was easy. But I had a feeling that would be the last straightforward part of this favor.

Proving my point, the Rickster said, "Now let me explain to you where the trip wire is so you don't disturb it."

I closed my eyes in exhaustion as I listened. *What have I gotten myself into?* I wondered.

Minutes later, with trip-wire directions fresh in my mind, I shoved the Rickster's key into my pocket and left the police station.

Outside, Callie and Owen stood in front of the station

again, back from their walk. They were facing each other and their body language was tense. I couldn't hear what they were saying, but the words were coming out fast and had a hissed quality to them.

Owen noticed me first. His eyes flashed down to Callie, and he said something. She whirled around, swiping tears from her cheeks.

"Hey!" she said way too cheerily. "You ready to go home? I'm totally ready to go." She practically jogged toward me, grasping my arm too tight and dragging me toward the car. She didn't even glance back at Owen.

But I did. His shoulders sagged unhappily, and he watched Callie sadly, as if she were walking out of his life forever.

9

"Callie, what's going on?" I asked once we were in the car.

She'd climbed into the driver's seat and practically peeled out of the marina parking lot.

"Nothing. Everything's fine." Even as she said the words, they wobbled in a very not fine way. "I'm just tired from paddleboarding. Being on the water, in the sun for that long, really tired me out. I think I just need to rest."

I narrowed my eyes at her, but I was feeling tired too. Being on the water for even a short time took more energy than I realized.

Once we got home, Callie locked herself in her room, saying she was going to take a nap, but I swear I heard sniffling sounds.

"Cal, you want anything for dinner?" I asked, standing outside her room a little while later.

"Not hungry. Thanks, though," she called out. I couldn't tell if her voice was muffled because of tears or the door between us.

Heading downstairs, I found Asher pacing in the tearoom. "Any luck?"

"Nope." I checked my watch. "I should get down to feed the Rickster's animals, but I don't want to leave in case she comes down and wants to talk."

Asher raised an eyebrow. "Puzzle while we wait?" he asked.

A lightness lifted my shoulders. I loved doing puzzles together. Normally, Asher would motion to the pieces, and I would click them into place, but with the jasper stones, he could probably pick them up himself.

"Let's do it." I smiled.

An entire puzzle later, it was officially dark outside.

I bit the inside of my cheek. "I don't think she's coming down. It's past her bedtime now."

Callie woke up a few hours earlier than me to prepare the baked items for our tea shop, which meant she usually went to bed hours before me as well.

Asher shook his head. "You should go feed the Rickster's pets before it gets too late." I must've glanced outside at the dark sky, because he added, "I'll be right there with you, if anything happens." He fixed me with a handsome smile.

Now that I had the moonstone ring and the ability to call Asher to me, even if he'd never set foot in a place while he was alive, he could come with me onto the Rickster's houseboat.

"Right." I swallowed, hoping I wouldn't need any saving.

And with that, we were off. Asher disappeared, and I drove into town. He met me at the dock, holding his hand up in a salute, knowing I would use the moonstone to call him to me once I was inside.

The scent of pitch stung at my nostrils as I walked down the dock toward the Rickster's houseboat. Boats groaned as they rubbed up against pilings, the gentle waves of the cove shifting them back and forth. The concrete and wood that had been baking in the scorching sun all day cooled in the night air. An eerie quiet surrounded me as I approached the dark houseboat.

The Rickster could've at least left on a couple of lights, I grumbled to myself.

Pulling out the key he'd given me, I stepped over the trip wire, unlocked the sliding door, and slipped inside, careful to lock it behind me.

The houseboat was small, snug, but clean. It smelled like coffee, a hint of mildew, and fresh wood shavings. The latter smell most likely came from the box in which the Rickster had taught both Atticus and Trickster to do their business. I wrinkled my nose at the bin but cleaned it out for the animals.

Just as I was raking the clean shavings back into place, I heard a sound. It could've been the splashing of a wave or the rustling of someone moving outside, but it got to me.

Twisting my moonstone ring so the large gemstone touched my thumb, I called Asher's name three times. He appeared in front of me, right in the middle of the Rickster's small couch. I sputtered out a laugh at the sight. Asher looked down, seeing half of his legs consumed by the piece of furniture. He chuckled and stepped forward.

Trickster scampered out from the bedroom first, his little

raccoon hands grabbing at my leg as he greeted me. Atticus waddled out after, quacking in a duckish hello.

"Hi, you two." I knelt to pet them, hoping they would remember me from the last time I was here. "Let's get you some food."

I followed the Rickster's instructions and found a premixed mush inside the small refrigerator. It was some sort of mixture of wet oats, peas, and grubs. My stomach turned, and I quickly set it down in front of the critters. After that, I gave them fresh drinking water and even changed out the water in the small wading pool the Rickster had set up in his shower for Atticus.

Once that was taken care of, I turned to Asher. He was taking in the space, eyes wide. I'd done the same thing the first time I'd stepped foot inside the Rickster's home. It felt like getting a behind-the-scenes look at a magic show, or maybe a fun house was more accurate.

Everything he owned seemed to be decorated in a unique pattern: plaid, floral, paisley, gingham, you name it; the Rickster had something in that print. That, plus the amount of stuff he'd crammed into the small space, contributed to a crowded, but cozy, atmosphere.

"I don't know what I expected, but …" Asher's words petered out.

I knew exactly what he was thinking. Somehow, this place was simultaneously exactly where I could picture the Rickster living while also being rather surprising. Asher and I locked eyes for a moment, sharing in the silliness of this window into the Rickster's world.

"Okay," I said. "Should we snoop?"

A sly smile pulled Asher's mouth up on one side. "Yes, and I can actually help this time."

Even though Ash was fairly transparent here, the jasper stones gave him the energy boost he needed. And while the stones allowed him minutes instead of seconds of energy use at a time, it definitely wasn't unlimited.

Asher picked up a piece of mail off the counter and looked at both sides.

I hummed. "I doubt a mooring bill is going to help us, though." The return address on the piece of mail said it was from the Pebble Cove Marina.

Asher wrinkled his nose and put it back. "True."

We kept searching.

"This might help," Ash said, holding up a different piece of mail.

Stepping closer, I studied the postcard along with him. It had a tropical view of a Hawaiian resort on one side. On the other side was a single sentence. *Wish you were here. - C*

"C? As in Captain?" I asked.

"Maybe." Asher shrugged and tucked the postcard back into the pile.

We noticed nothing else of interest during the rest of our searching. Remembering the Rickster's worries about a killer lurking around his houseboat, my skin itched to get out of there. But the moment I moved toward the door, Trickster stopped eating and grabbed at my legs, as if he were begging me to stay longer. The poor things must've been starved for attention with the Rickster gone.

"I should stick around for a little longer," I said, my heart melting as the raccoon grabbed ahold of my hand.

Asher chuckled but took a seat as I curled up on the

small plaid couch in the tiny living room. Atticus quacked and waddled off into the bedroom, but Trickster curled up in my lap like a cat. His little humanlike hands played with the ends of my shoulder-length hair. It was rather adorable.

Until he stopped, his gaze moving to the large sliding door on the other side of the houseboat. He tipped his head, like he heard something we didn't. My heart beat faster, but the raccoon went back to playing with my hair.

"You're sure the Rickster's trip wire will work?" Asher whispered even though I was the only one who could hear him.

"About as sure as I am about anything to do with the Rickster," I answered.

"Which is to say, not very." Asher chuckled. "And what does it do to alert us?"

"Makes a quacking sound, like Atticus." I winced as Trickster pulled a little too hard on my hair. Prying the strands from his grasp, I let him curl his fingers around my index finger instead.

Asher waited and listened. Living on a houseboat came with a lot of unfamiliar sounds. While in our house, we were used to the creaky stairs, the groans that the old wood floors let out in certain areas, the constant sound of the waves in the background, and the wind chimes in the garden.

The sounds here were different but equally constant. The houseboat groaned a little each time it rocked with the gentle waves. Something on a nearby boat flapped in the wind. And the waves splashed as they lapped up onto the sides of the dock.

I frowned as something new was added to the sound-track. It was a low rumble, almost like … I looked down and realized it was coming from my lap. Trickster was fast asleep, snoring, head resting on my arm.

Relief enveloped me as the threat of an intruder drifted away. When I glanced up, Asher was studying me. His eyes were crinkled at the corners and his mouth pulled into the slightest of smiles.

I cleared my throat. "So ..." I started, hoping a conversation might distract me from thoughts of kissing him again.

But for the first time in a long time, I couldn't think of what to say to my best friend. If I brought up his murder, I'd have to come clean about learning about Lyle, and who knew if that was going to be the ultimate piece that clicked into place for Asher.

I could see it now. His expression would darken at the name Lyle, and he might say something like, *"I can't believe I hadn't thought of him before. Of course, he would've wanted me out of the way."* And it could all be over, just like that.

"What do you think is going on with Callie?" I asked, choosing a safer topic.

Asher's gaze moved up to the ceiling like he was thinking through all of his recent interactions with her. "I didn't notice anything before today. But you're right. Locking herself in her room for a whole evening isn't like her. You said she got in a fight with Owen?"

I nodded slowly, unsure. "That's what it looked like. I'm not sure what it was about or why she feels she can't tell me."

"Maybe it's about you," Asher said quietly. It wasn't a mean statement or meant to make me feel badly. It was simply the truth, something I hadn't considered until he said it.

Now it was my turn to think through all of my recent interactions with her. "Maybe. I have been preoccupied lately. I'll ask her tomorrow."

We sat in awkward silence for a moment.

"Rosie," Ash said. He opened his mouth to say more, but a loud quacking startled me into silence. Asher and I stood. Trickster jumped out of my lap.

"The signal," I whispered to Asher.

He disappeared, going outside to check around the boat for intruders. I tried to listen past the duck quacking in order to pick up sounds of someone trying to break in, but it was too loud. Was there a way to turn it off? I wished I'd thought to ask the Rickster.

Heading into the bedroom, toward the sound, I figured I could find the device and turn it off. But when I walked into the Rickster's small bedroom, I found Atticus walking around, quacking loudly.

It was the actual duck, not the alarm.

How did the Rickster ever figure out if it was a trip wire or his actual pet duck making the noise? It would make me completely on edge and paranoid … just like the Rickster. I almost wanted to laugh, but Asher appeared inside, his jaw clenched tight.

"I can't see anyone." His eyes flicked through the small space.

I motioned to the duck waddling from the bedroom, finally quiet. "It was just Atticus. He must've had a bad dream or something." I wrinkled my nose. "Do ducks dream?"

Asher shrugged. Trickster moved to the bedroom and

snuggled up with Atticus on the Rickster's bed. I let out a long yawn and checked my watch.

"I think that's my sign to head home," I said. "Thanks for being my backup."

"Anytime." Asher smiled.

I locked up, heading for home. But I couldn't stop my thoughts from returning to the moment Asher had been interrupted by Atticus's quacking. I wasn't sure if I was strong enough to hear what he'd been about to say.

10

I covered my mouth and let out another yawn the next morning.

Callie poked me in the side. "That's the third time in the last ten minutes. Why don't you go take a nap? I've got the teahouse covered." She waved toward to the tearoom, which was about halfway full.

The sun was shining, and while our iced tea selection brought just as many customers in on hot days as our cozy hot teas did during the stormy ones, Mondays usually weren't too busy. The knitting club would come soon, but other than that, it would likely remain on the sleepy side, like me. Callie could definitely handle it on her own.

She'd been back to her normal self in the morning, brushing aside my worries. "I was just tired," she'd said when I'd repeated my questions of concern from the night before.

Asher's comment about the thing that was bothering her possibly being me, stuck in my brain. What if she was mad that I'd been leaving so much? Granted, that had been more prevalent months ago when we were prepping for Mom's wedding and helping a ghost move on, but maybe she felt like it was going to happen again with this recent case? Did she feel left out? I made a promise to myself to find out.

"I'm okay," I said, giving her two thumbs-up, hoping it would convince her. "Here, let me help you with that." I gestured to the handful of dishes she was carting back to the tea bar.

Together, we got the dishes loaded into the dishwasher and were all ready for more tables. The knitters arrived soon after, Keller and some of his crew following closely on their heels.

Callie headed for the knitters and took their orders while I focused on the fishermen.

"What can I get started for you?" I asked Keller, turning on a kettle of hot water.

Keller waved his hands to stop me. "We're not staying, Rosie. I just wanted to pick up a bag of the Fisherman's blend, and the boys wanted to get some pastries to go."

"Jolene's place is much closer to the marina," I said warily. They could've picked up both things at her location downtown.

Keller rubbed the back of his neck uncomfortably. "I know. It's just ... the boys wanted ..." He cleared his throat. "We don't have time to get roped into a conversation about that stand-up paddleboarding she's always going on about lately."

I bit back a laugh, nodding in understanding. "What can I get you to eat?" I asked Keller's crew.

I bagged up their bakery items, handing them over along with a bag of the Fisherman's blend black tea.

"Where are you off to today?" I asked, always fascinated by the fishing trade and the dangerous job they had.

Keller leaned his forearms on the tea bar. "Just a quick trip up to Astoria," he said. "Need to pick up our crab pots. We store 'em up there in the off season."

I pushed my shoulders back at the mention of Astoria. If I truly wanted to look into who could've wanted Captain dead, that would be a good place to start. Not that I didn't trust the chief to find out the correct information, it was just that I had an advantage because the list of people I could question included spirits.

Callie walked behind me to reach the scones, plating a few for the knitters. "Astoria, huh?" Callie asked, the question loaded. She spilled some of her intention when she added, "Rosemary's been talking about wanting to visit."

I narrowed my eyes at her, not sure where she was going with this.

Keller's face brightened. "Oh, it's a great place. You should definitely visit if you haven't been before. The best experience is by boat, if you ask me. Going over the bar is still exhilarating, even though I've done it so many times."

"The bar?" I asked.

"The place where the Columbia River meets the Pacific Ocean. It's one of the most dangerous spots on the West Coast. It can create thirty-foot swells out of nowhere that'll swallow a boat whole if you're not careful." Even though that sounded terrifying, Keller's eyes flashed with excitement. "They don't call it the Graveyard of the Pacific for nothing." He chuckled, then must've noticed my pale expression. "It's not too bad if you're with someone who knows what he's doing, like me." He jabbed his thumb at his chest. "If you ever want to catch a ride with us, we'd love to have you."

"How long are you going to be gone for?" I asked.

"Just the day," Keller said, checking his watch. "Leaving in about an hour. It'll take us a few hours to load the pots, and then we'll be coming back this evening."

Callie nudged me with her elbow from behind. "You should go," she said.

I exhaled a laugh. "Good one."

"No, I'm serious." She leaned forward so she could meet my gaze. "I can hold down the tea shop. Check out the city." She said the last sentence with a particular amount of emphasis, telling me she thought I should do some research while I was there.

I couldn't tell which research she meant, though: Asher's family business or Captain's. I supposed I could do both if I used my time efficiently.

Studying Callie, I thought about the possibility that I'd offended her by leaving her out of investigations. She'd never been all that involved in my investigation into Asher, so Riley and I taking over most of the research didn't seem like it would upset her. But maybe she was mad she hadn't been more involved in the Rickster and Captain Westover case.

"Why don't you come along?" I suggested. "We can close the shop for a day. It might be fun." My eyes pored over her face, trying to glean even the smallest sign that me leaving her behind was the source of her frustration.

But Callie's expression crumpled into a scowl. "Oh, no thank you. I'm happy staying here."

She said it with such finality, and then walked away with

the tea for the knitters, that I couldn't argue. It was then that I remembered her last trip on a boat wasn't exactly fun. *Great, Rosemary. No wonder she's mad at you when you say inconsiderate stuff like that.*

Keller watched me expectantly.

"Okay, I guess I'm going to tag along with you to Astoria. I'll meet you down at the boat in a half hour. Let me just get myself organized. I'll see you at the marina," I said, excitement quickening the pace of my sentences.

Keller gave me a two-fingered salute. The fishermen headed out in a group.

I padded upstairs, looking for some privacy from customers, and called Asher to me. He appeared, looking more than a little stunned that I'd summoned him to my bedroom. My cheeks grew hot, and I said, "I'm going to Astoria with Keller to do a little research. Want to come with?" I asked. "I can call you there once we arrive. Unless you want to ride on the boat too."

Asher's mouth worked from side to side for a moment. "I haven't been on a boat in a while." He adopted an excited, boyish grin.

I smiled too. "Keller said crossing the bar is really interesting and dangerous, so I'd say we're in for a treat."

———

THE SALTY SEA air thumped against my chest, almost stealing my breath and pushing me back onto my heels. It hadn't even been windy on the beach, but once we got out of the cove and started picking up knots, the gusts were vicious. And that was before we even approached the bar, that infamous section where the river met the ocean.

Leading up to the bar, there was so much chatter about favorable breezes, timing our arrival with the slack tide, currents, buoys, and swells, that I eventually tuned out the crew, not understanding half of what they were saying. But all the preparations made sense once we went through the dreaded section. Even though the crew was entirely capable, it was a rough ride. There seemed to be dangers at every turn.

To cement the precariousness of our situation, Coast Guard boats were out at Cape Disappointment, practicing lifesaving maneuvers, the kind I hoped I would never have to see up close. One Coast Guard vessel was even escorting a recreational boat over the bar since, in Keller's assessment, it was pretty nasty today.

Keller didn't seem flustered one bit as he navigated the choppy channel, but I couldn't say the same about myself. The trip gave me a severe case of seasickness. The feeling didn't subside once we were on the river, chugging over calm waters up the ten-mile stretch to Astoria.

"A treat, huh?" Asher said as he sidled up next to me where I clung to the railing of Keller's boat.

I groaned. "I've lived by the sea for over two years at this point. I thought I was a sea person." I clutched my stomach with the hand that wasn't gripping the boat.

"You say something there, Rosie?" one fisherman called to me.

I turned around and waved weakly. "Just grumbling to myself."

The fisherman chuckled and nodded. "Okay, don't worry. You'll get your sea legs soon."

"I think it's becoming very clear that you're a *by* the sea person. Not an *on* the sea person," Asher clarified with a laugh.

As terrible as I felt, it was nice to joke around with him. I was glad he'd come. I thought back to Callie's suggestion to savor the moments we had together, and I knew today was something I'd write about in the journal I'd started. The crew was busy enough that they left me alone, other than the occasional check-in, and I was free to chat with Asher for the remainder of the trip.

We pulled into Astoria a while later, the iconic bridge spanning the width of the river, providing a link between Oregon and Washington.

Keller helped me off the boat once we docked. "We're going to be loading pots most of the day if you want to walk around." He pointed to a large storage area behind the fish market. "We'll be setting out at seven sharp." He checked his watch, and I knew that timing was important, planned out to a T, so we could catch the tides correctly for another safe passage over the bar.

"Sounds good. I've got your number." I shook my phone in the air.

Walking away from the docks, I pulled up an internet search on my phone and looked up Cap's Sail Loft. The map told me it was only a few blocks' walk from where I was. Asher had stayed behind on the boat, but the plan was for me to call him once I arrived.

The streets of Astoria were adorable. A river walk took

me down the main business section, which held a lot of the typical seaside fare. There were ice cream parlors, cute coffee shops, and souvenir stalls that made me want to stop and look around. But I was working on a fixed timeline today, and I wanted to make sure I got as much information as I could before I had to meet the crew back at the boat later.

I found Captain's business easily enough. The sail loft was contained in a large warehouse at the other end of the river walk, past the touristy shops, closer to the industrial part of the city.

Once I was in front of the sail loft, I called Asher to me, breathing a sigh of relief when he showed up by my side. After years of being constrained by where he had been during his lifetime, it was still sinking in that I could call him to me anywhere I needed to go now. And each time I did it, I semi-expected it not to work.

"Ready?" Asher asked, eyeing the building.

"As I'll ever be. Let's hope we get some answers," I said, taking a tentative step inside the building.

But as Asher walked forward, he stopped, as if an invisible wall had knocked him on his heels. I took a step back, so I was outside again. Swallowing hard, I asked, "Can't you enter?"

He shook his head. "Something's stopping me from going in."

11

—————

"What do you mean, something's stopping you?" I whispered, stepping away from the door to the sail loft and looking back at Asher.

"It's like there's an invisible wall." He studied the exterior of the building, like the sign out front or the metal siding might hold the answers we needed.

"Maybe it's because I summoned you when we were outside," I thought aloud. "I can step inside and try it."

Asher nodded, but there was a tightness to his expression that made me more worried than I wanted to admit.

I entered, stepping into a retail space. A chill washed over me like I'd just walked through a ghost, but there weren't any spirits that I could see. It was just me and a saleswoman inside the small space. There were fabric samples, order books, and pictures of sailboats. Large windows lined the back wall, giving a clear view inside a huge warehouse space behind. Expansive tables for cutting and sewing sails sat in the middle of industrial shelving units holding rolls of fabric and other necessary materials.

There had to be at least fifty people working in the large warehouse area. To my left there was an office. The saleswoman sat at a desk; two chairs sat opposite her, for ordering, I guessed.

"Welcome in. Can I help you with anything?" the woman asked. She was older, and her tanned skin made it clear she'd spent many of her years out in the sun.

"Just browsing," I said, cramming my hands into my pockets.

She smiled at me, her skin wrinkling like old leather as she did so. I wandered over to a display listing the different sails they made, pretending to be perusing the merchandise. Once I was far enough away from the woman, I swiveled my moonstone ring and placed my thumb on the stone before whispering Asher's full name three times. I waited.

Nothing.

Glancing outside, I could see him standing in front of the building. He shook his head.

I moved to leave but stopped myself. Rushing out of the shop after I'd only just arrived would definitely seem suspicious. Pulling out my phone, I pretended to answer a call.

"Hi. How are you?" I said to no one. Then, making a show of frowning, I added, "Hold on, I can barely hear you. Let me step outside." Looking over at the woman behind the desk, I held up a finger to show her I would be back after I took this call.

Keeping the phone to my ear so it wouldn't seem like I was talking to myself, I walked outside, moving around the corner of the building. Asher followed.

"What should we do?" I asked him once I could no longer see the front door of the sail loft.

Asher raised his palms. "I've never encountered this before."

Remembering the chill that had washed over my skin when I'd first gone inside, I said, "I wonder if there's some kind of curse on the building." I thought through who I could ask for advice. Normally, I would run things by our local ghosts. I supposed I could call one of them to me or have Asher travel back to Pebble Cove to ask them.

"You can go inside," he said, gesturing to the building. "I can just wait out here for you."

"But you're a big part of the snooping plan. Plus, don't you think we should figure this out?" I spun the moonstone ring on my finger as I thought.

At the third turn, my fingers froze as I remembered the shop where I'd bought the moonstone ring.

"Destiny," I said, pushing my shoulders back. "I could call her." We'd met the herbal witch during our last investigation, and she'd introduced us to the magic of gemstones.

Asher nodded, and I brought my phone away from my ear for a moment so I could look up the number to her shop in Sun City.

"Hi, Rosemary," Destiny said as she answered the phone. No business greeting or anything.

I sucked in a surprised inhale. "Did you sense it was me calling?"

She chuckled. "Sure, or it could've been the caller ID. We exchanged numbers last time you were in, remember?"

"Oh, right." My shoulders dropped an inch or two from the disappointment. "Hey, I have a question."

"Ask away," she said.

"Why would I not be able to call Asher into a certain

building, even with a moonstone? Do you think there could be a curse on the place? It's like he's hitting an invisible wall, and I can't call him inside." I kept twirling my ring as I spoke.

Destiny was silent for a moment on the other end of the call.

"Are you still there?" I asked. "Did I lose you?"

"I'm here." Destiny cleared her throat. "It's not a curse, but if I were you, I'd get out of there, Rosemary." Her voice was strangled, as if someone had their hands around her throat.

An icy chill settled on the back of my neck and slid down my spine. I took a step back. Asher did the same, putting himself in between me and the building.

"Why? What is it?" I asked, my voice rising in pitch as my anxiety grew.

"If Asher can't enter, but you can, it means there's likely a spirit that's blocking him specifically," Destiny explained. "It could be a soul that blocks all ghosts, or it could be one who's mad at Asher. And while they can't hurt him, they could direct their anger toward you and become violent."

I shivered away the chill that had moved to my limbs. "Violent?" I took another step away from the building.

"Yes, I would leave, if I were you," she reiterated.

Asher frowned as he studied me. His eyes flicked over my features, trying to read my expression for clues as to what Destiny was saying.

Surveying the building, I grimaced. Who here might be mad at Asher? He'd never been to Astoria before. Plus, this building was crawling with people. The spirit who was stopping Asher from entering wouldn't hurt me in front of all the workers inside. Would they? The question made my stomach flip with unease, but I needed to get inside and ask about Captain if I had any chance of solving his murder.

"Okay, thanks, Destiny," I said. She didn't need to know that I still planned on entering.

"At least take some salt with you if you enter," she added.

Of course she could read my mind. The woman was clairvoyant. She'd known Callie and I were mediums the moment we'd set foot in her shop. Her knowledge of salt didn't shock me either. She'd known about the powers of gemstones in the hands of ghosts, so she would know about the power of salt. But I hadn't had cause to carry salt in months, and I certainly didn't have any with me now.

I bit my lip. "Will do."

We hung up. I kept the phone pressed against my face so I could talk to Asher.

"She thinks I should grab some salt, just in case. What should we do?" I asked, conflicted.

On one hand, I only had so many hours here in Astoria —Keller and his crew would take off after dinner. Going somewhere to buy salt seemed like a waste of time. On the other hand, I'd met a couple of angry, belligerent spirits in my time, and I wasn't looking forward to adding another one to the list. I'd never been hurt by one, but there was a first time for everything.

Asher paced, seeming to understand the quandary. "You didn't see any spirits while you were in there?"

"There was only one saleswoman inside the retail space, but there were a bunch of workers in the warehouse." My eyes widened. "Maybe one of them is the ghost."

Asher ran a hand through his hair in frustration. "I'll support whatever you want to do; just know I won't be able to come in and help you."

"I know. I want to try again. I'll be careful." I pulled in a deep breath, preparing myself.

Asher's dark eyebrows were furrowed so tightly that the crease between them showed up. "Get out of there the moment something doesn't feel right."

"I will." Moving around the corner of the building, I headed for the front door once more.

When I pulled it open, I noticed two people must've entered while I'd been on the phone with Destiny. One was a middle-aged man. Between the shorts, boat shoes, and polo he wore, I could see he was the typical sailor type. The other person was an older man who wore jean overalls and a white Henley. He appeared to be someone who might work on boats rather than sail them, but from the assured way he strode through the shop, he seemed to know what he was looking for.

I walked toward the desk. But before I could reach it, the older man got in line in front of me, facing the woman behind the desk. She wasn't paying attention to him, however, paging through a magazine instead. I guess without Captain Westover, there was no boss anymore, no one to tell her not to slack off.

I lined up behind the man in the overalls, and we waited for the woman to notice us. I was just about to cough to get her attention when a man about my age walked through the office door and into the retail space. He grabbed a binder off one of the display tables.

"Gloria, look alive," he said as his eyes flicked from the

line of customers back to her before he disappeared back into the office.

The woman named Gloria glanced up. "Oh, I'm so sorry. How can I help you?" Even though the man was clearly first in line, she stared directly at me. "May I help you, ma'am?"

I pointed toward the man. "He was here first, actually."

The woman followed the line of my finger but looked right through the man in overalls like she couldn't see him. "Who?" She looked behind me at the middle-aged sailor in boat shoes. "I don't think he's in line. I can help you if you'd like to step forward."

It was then that everything clicked. I'd found the ghost.

Seeing as how I couldn't very well step around the overall-wearing spirit in front of me, I braced myself and walked straight through him toward the desk. A chill washed through me, and I risked a glance back at him.

The spirit's gaze caught on to mine, and I knew I'd made a terrible mistake.

12

————————

"How can I help you today?" Gloria asked, her voice just as scratchy and weathered as her skin. She motioned for me to sit across from her.

I plopped into a chair and opened my mouth, but before I could say anything, the overall-wearing spirit raced toward me. I schooled my expression, working hard not to flinch as he planted himself in front of me.

"You can see me. I know you can," he said. "You thought I was in line." He pointed a ghostly finger at me. Well, it wasn't ghostly at all. He looked as real as Gloria did to me. I hadn't doubted for one second that he was anything other than solid.

Unease skittered up the backs of my arms. Destiny's words about the ghost protecting this building possibly being violent came to mind. Weighing my two options, I decided I was less likely to get hurt if I continued to pretend he wasn't there.

I ignored him and focused on Gloria. "Actually, I'm

searching for information about Captain Westover. Is there someone who could tell me more about him?"

"Come on," the ghost flashed a gap-toothed grin at me as he craned his neck so he was mere inches from my face. "I swear you saw me."

It took all of my concentration to act as if he wasn't there—especially since his spirit was so strong that I couldn't see through him. My hard work paid off and the ghost stepped back, his hopeful posture deflating as his gaze dropped.

"I guess I was wrong," he mumbled.

Mirroring the ghost's feelings, Gloria's expression dropped. "Oh, love. I hate to have to break this to you, but Captain's passed on. I'm so sorry."

Passed on seemed like a really gentle way to describe being stabbed to death, but I didn't press my luck.

I blinked. After feeling seasick all morning, the disequilibrium hung about me like a rain cloud. "Oh, I know," I said, unable to hide the truth. "I'm sorry. To clarify, I'm hoping someone can talk to me about his death." I pushed back my shoulders, willing this woman to talk to me about her boss.

She set her elbows on the desk in front of her. "You a journalist?"

The overall-wearing spirit wandered away, staring out the windows at the river.

Focusing my attention back on the woman, I shrugged. "A journalist? Uh ... something like that."

Gloria relaxed. "The detective that came by yesterday mostly talked to Matt." Gloria hooked her thumb toward the office door. "I won't be offended if you want to talk to him. He's the one that knew Cap's schedule in and out."

Ah, so the man who'd come out of the office had been Matt, Captain's assistant. And the detective she'd mentioned must've been Chief Clemenson. I realized that not everyone was as up on the difference between detectives and police chiefs, but that was okay.

"I'd love to speak with Matt, but I'd also like to talk to you." I leaned forward.

If Gloria had feathers, she would've fluffed them out at this compliment. "Sure. Ask away."

"Was there anyone who might have reason to want him dead?" I asked.

Gloria shook her head. "Not that I can think of, and believe me, I've been racking my brain since we got the news. Everyone loved Cap."

"That's what it sounds like." As I said that, the office door opened again.

"Oh, Matt. This young lady would like to ask you some questions about Cap, if you have a second," Gloria said. "She's a journalist."

Matt's gaze flicked up to meet mine as he returned the binder to the display table. "Sure. I've got something I'm working on in the office. We can talk in there."

I nodded and glanced behind me at the front windows where I knew Asher was waiting. I pointed to the office, letting him know I would be going inside so he didn't worry. Asher gave me a tight nod that told me he was definitely still going to worry. When I turned back to follow Matt, the overall-wearing ghost's eyes were wide. His gaze flicked from

Asher to me and back again. Inhaling, I turned away as quickly as I could.

But it was too late.

"Ah-ha!" He raced forward. "I knew it. You *can* see me."

I slipped into the office after Matt, and the door closed behind me. I bit back a groan as the ghost walked right through the door. Still, my fear about a violent spirit lessened. He didn't seem angry. Annoying? Yes. But not upset.

"So … what do you want to know?" Matt asked. Between the stacks of papers in front of him on the desk and the open binders, it looked like he was doing some overdue organizing. A poster on the wall held a red sign with a white diagonal line through it. I recognized it as the scuba diving flag. The air tank Asher and I found came to mind.

Interest piqued, I pointed to the symbol. "Do you dive?" I asked.

Matt's gaze flicked over to the framed flag. "Cap did. He did everything."

Captain was a diver? That didn't help explain the tank we'd found in the cove.

I cleared my throat, getting back on track. "Do you know of anyone who might've had an issue with him or want to kill him?"

Matt stopped what he was doing, setting the papers down on the desk. He pinched at the bridge of his nose. "I've been staying up at night thinking of this, but honestly, there isn't anyone I can think of. Everyone loved Cap. He was like a grandfather to me."

I wrinkled my nose in frustration. If the people closest to him didn't have any leads, how was this case going to get solved at all? And if it didn't, it seemed like the Rickster was on the hook for the murder.

The ghost, who'd been pacing behind Matt while he and I talked, stopped and locked eyes with me. I fought hard to stare past him.

That became almost impossible when the ghost said, "Look, I know something about Cap's death. And I'll tell you all about it. All I need you to do is admit you can see me." The ghost narrowed his eyes and studied me.

As tempting as that offer sounded, I couldn't tell if the spirit was making it up to get me to talk. Also, if he was the one who'd blocked Asher from coming into the building, I wasn't sure he was the kind of spirit I wanted to be conversing with. Sure, he hadn't become violent yet, but that didn't mean he wouldn't.

I focused on Matt. "I saw he traveled a lot. Is it possible he got into some trouble on one of his trips?" I asked, thinking back to the postcard from Captain in the Rickster's houseboat.

Matt rubbed his palm over his clean-shaven chin. "The man was a seasoned traveler. I went with him on the last few trips, and he basically just made friends wherever he went."

I curled my fingers into fists on top of my thighs as I thought of other options.

Matt's expression softened. "Look, I know it sounds crazy, but the guy really was the best. He's really going to be missed." He peered around like he was making sure no one slipped inside the small office without his noticing while we'd been talking. "I don't know how accurate this is, but I heard a rumor that an old buddy of his lives in Pebble Cove, where he was killed. I'd put my money on that guy."

Any hope I had deflated. The Rickster. I was back at the beginning.

"What makes you think his old friend did it?" I asked. "I thought you said everyone loved Captain."

"Sure, but someone as dynamic and successful as Captain ... Maybe this friend was jealous of him. It sounds like he's going to inherit the company, so there was a motive for him to get Cap out of the way." Matt shrugged as if to say *that theory isn't without its issues, but it's the best I've got.*

The pacing ghost finally got fed up and yelled out, "Liar! There is someone you're not talking about." He pointed to Matt, then turned back to me. "Ask him about the seaplane! He'll have to tell you the truth about the seaplane."

Seeing myself at a dead end otherwise, I gave in to the ghost's demands.

"What about the seaplane? That could be something, right?" I asked, trying to sound like I knew more than I did about the incident.

"The seaplane?" Matt's face went slack, like he was having a revelation. "You're right. I totally forgot about that." He studied something off in the distance.

The ghost crossed his arms in smug triumph. "I knew it," he said.

My mention of the seaplane had gotten Matt thinking, and he started rambling. "Cap was really cryptic when it happened. I just assumed it was because he was tired and didn't want to discuss it, but maybe it's because he was shaken. And then there was that meeting on his schedule with that random lawyer." Matt raked his hands through his hair, in a way that spoke of the turmoil he was feeling at the possibility that his beloved boss could've done something bad. He turned to me. "How'd you hear about the seaplane incident?"

I curled my fingers into fists as I thought of an answer. I glanced over at the ghost to see if he had any suggestions, but he merely smiled at me, like he was enjoying watching me struggle.

"I can't say." I cringed in apology. "Gotta keep my sources a secret, you know." I rolled my eyes, as if the rules of journalism applied to me at all.

Matt accepted that and went back to being flabbergasted. "I can't believe I didn't think of that."

I nodded, but a bitter sense of dread filled me as I realized the failure in this plan. By pretending I knew all about this alleged seaplane incident, I had closed the door on the possibility of Matt explaining the incident to me.

I shot a quick glare over at the ghost standing in the corner of the room. He'd better know what he was talking about or else I was officially out of leads.

13

Checking my watch, I told Matt that I needed to get going to follow another story lead. I sure was clinging to this fake journalist angle.

"I don't suppose you have a card, if I have any further questions," I asked tentatively.

Matt dug into the desk drawer in front of him. "Yeah, absolutely. I'd be happy to help."

Matt's card in hand, I headed out into the salesroom. Asher was plastered up against the window, eyes searching for me. His hard glare softened as the office door closed behind me. I figured the overall-wearing ghost would follow me, but once I got outside, the only spirit standing with me was Asher.

Frowning, I motioned for Ash to follow me around the side of the building where we'd called Destiny so we could talk freely. I was about to spill everything that had happened inside when a face appeared in the building's siding to my right.

I screamed and jumped back. It was the overall-wearing

spirit, but only his face. Nothing else showed. Luckily, no one else was around, because I don't think I would've had the wherewithal to hold a phone to my ear at that point.

"What are you doing?" I hissed at the ghost.

"Is this the ghost responsible?" Asher asked, pushing back his shoulders.

"Yep," I confirmed.

The spirit's attention flicked between me and Asher. Fear shone behind his eyes as Asher approached him. A hand appeared from the side of the building, held out flat like a stop sign. "The ghost responsible for what? I didn't do anything."

"You blocked me from going inside." Asher practically growled the words. "I was forced to wait out here, worried Rosie was in danger the whole time."

"That wasn't me," the ghost said, cutting the air with his palm. "It was probably the other spirit who haunts this place. He's terribly grumpy. Lives inside the walls." His eyes traveled in an arc as he studied the wall around him.

Asher relaxed. "Then who are you, and why are you following Rosie?"

The ghost held a hand forward and said, "The name's Trip Stevens. Ex-pilot."

"You flew planes?" I asked in surprise. I'd just assumed he was a sailor or fisherman, living so close to the Columbia River.

Asher shook his head at the same time Trip snorted.

"No," Trip said in disgust, like flying planes was child's play.

"Pilots are people who guide boats through the treach-erous passageway over the bar, and sometimes farther up or down the coast or river," Asher explained patiently to me. "They're a very skilled minority." He appraised what was visible of Trip's spirit with a newfound respect.

"Oh, like the Coast Guard we saw leading that boat in?" I asked.

Asher nodded. "Sometimes they use pilot boats to lead other boats to safety," Asher explained. "Other times pilots ride on the boat itself to wherever the next port is, and then catch a ride back with another boat."

Now it was Trip's turn to appraise Asher with respect. "The kid knows his stuff," he said, confirming that Asher had been right about his profession.

"But if you weren't the spirit who stopped Asher from coming inside just now, why were you bothering me in there?" I asked.

Trip's eyes widened. "I'm lonely. I haven't had any visitors in a really long time. I got excited. It's difficult when you're stuck in one place." His gaze shifted down to the ground, dropping with his tone.

"You're stuck here?" Asher asked.

Trip nodded. "Never been able to leave. I see other spirits walking around, so I'm not sure what my problem is. I showed up here after I died and haven't left since."

I cut my eyes to Asher just as he glanced at me. Maybe it wasn't just Asher who couldn't enter the building. It was possible that the spirit had blocked any ghost from coming or going. We shared a quick nonverbal conversation, agreeing that I should try to help.

"Trip, do you want me to help you get out of there?" I asked tentatively.

His brown eyes lit up. "You would do that for me?"

Softening toward the previously annoying spirit, I said, "Of course. Just give me your full name."

Studying me with increasing interest, he said, "Daniel Trip Stevens. My middle name comes from my grandpa." He beamed.

Twirling my ring so I could set my thumb on the cool moonstone, I said his name three times. We waited.

Trip didn't move. His face and hands remained where they were, stuck in the building's siding.

"Maybe you're too close," Asher said.

I took a few steps back. Then I tried it again. Still nothing.

Trip's mouth pulled down on one side. "That's okay. Thanks for trying, though. Being stuck here's not so bad, really. I love watching them make the sails."

I paced, not willing to give up as easily as he was. "Maybe it has something to do with your unfinished business," I suggested. "Do you know why your spirit is still here, Trip?"

Surprising both me and Asher, Trip said, "Oh, yeah. I know. It's because my best buddy, Hank, is waiting for me." Seeing the interest seeping from our body language, Trip elaborated. "I was a pilot. He was a coastie. We made a pact to never leave the other behind. But one day, we were supposed to meet up at The Astoria Column on Coxcomb Hill. He never showed. Turned out that he went under during a rescue. I bet he's waiting at the column for me right now. I just haven't been able to figure out a way up there." He gestured to the hill behind us.

I remembered Keller and his crew telling me about the structure during the boat ride here. The hundred- and twenty-five-foot tower was a monument to the natural riches of the Pacific Northwest and the people who settled there.

Sucking in a quick breath, I said, "We won't give up. I'll do some research and see if I can help you. There has to be a way for you to find Hank and move on together."

Trip's eyes grew big and glassy. "Thank you."

"So what can you tell me about the seaplane incident?" I asked.

Trip puffed out his cheeks. "Not much, unfortunately."

My excitement sank into disappointment.

Sensing my frustration, Trip kept talking. "Captain came back one day visibly shaken. He'd been out on his boat, and when Matt asked what was wrong, he said there had been some sort of situation with a seaplane. He wouldn't talk about it other than that." Trip cocked his head to one side.

"When was this?" I asked.

"About a month ago?" Trip squinted one eye. "Maybe less."

"Oh." My tone went flat. Vague dates and half stories would not give me the answers I needed.

Then Trip said, "I don't remember the date exactly, but I remember the name."

I perked up.

"Joseph Fairhaven. Cap had it written on a card that he stuffed into his wallet when he got back." Trip scratched at his forehead.

Pulling out my phone, I typed in the name. Joseph owned a small art studio about a mile up the hill. I glanced behind me, knowing I was without a car and would have to walk.

"We'd better get going, then," Asher said. "We don't

want to be late for our ride back," he added, rubbing at the base of his neck.

But we had hours until we needed to be back at the boat. Even with the long walk to Joseph's studio, we would have plenty of time to make it back to Keller and his crew. Which meant that Asher wanted to do something else while we were here. He wanted to look into his family business, I realized.

Before Trip could leave, I said, "One more thing."

He blinked back at me. "Yeah?"

"The Benson Fishing Company," I said, noticing how Asher's posture stiffened eagerly at the mention of his family's business. "Do you know it? It was based here in Astoria before the Great Depression."

Trip's nose twitched. "Doesn't ring a bell. I started here in the fifties, though." His eyes lit up. "But you know where they would have information about that? The Columbia River Maritime Museum." He pointed behind us. "Opened in the sixties. It's a wealth of information about the boating and shipping industries. It's a huge building. You can't miss it."

"Oh, thank you," I said, monitoring Asher's reaction in my peripheral vision.

His entire face was alight, but there was a hint of apprehension. The feelings swirling around inside me were just as confusing.

"We'll make that our next stop," I promised.

I stuffed down the fear that even stepping foot in that maritime museum could mean I had to say goodbye to my best friend. "Right. It was great to meet you, Trip. Thank you for your help. We'll get you out of there. I promise."

"The pleasure's all mine," he said before disappearing into the building.

We started walking toward Joseph's studio, eager to learn what we could about him and his run-in with Captain. While I had it on my mind, I texted Destiny, asking her for advice with Trip's conundrum. The message sent, I slipped my phone back into my pocket. Ash and I moved in silence, not sure what to say to each other.

Just as we were approaching the address for the studio a short while later, my phone rang. Hope gripped at my chest. Maybe it would be Keller telling me they were ready to leave. I could pop in, ask Joseph about the seaplane incident, and we wouldn't have time to learn anything more about Asher's family business on this trip. I could drive up at a different time, when I was ready—whenever that might be.

But the name on my phone wasn't Keller's. It was the chief's. I stopped walking to answer the call.

"Hi, Raymond," I said, surprise coating my words.

"Rosie, I just heard you're up in Astoria." His words were coated in something more like suspicion.

Biting my lip for a second, I grimaced. "Oh ... I ... uh ..."

"You wouldn't be looking into this case, would you?" he asked, his tone a terrifying mixture of stern police chief and disappointed father.

"Why would you think that?" I asked around the frog in my throat.

"Because the Rickster just told me he hired you to look into this case for him," Raymond said flatly.

"Hired?" I blurted. "I didn't know I was getting paid for

this." I realized my mistake all too late. Asher closed his eyes.

"Ah-ha. Gotcha." The chief snapped his fingers in the background.

"Okay, okay," I admitted. "I might be asking around while I'm here. I promise I'm being careful," I said, then realized that what I'd learned at the sail loft might get me out of trouble. "I also may have stumbled upon a lead."

"Oh?" Raymond asked, proving I knew him well.

"Captain Westover had an 'incident' with a seaplane and a man named Joseph Fairhaven about a month before he was killed. Matt seemed to think Cap was upset about the situation, and that it may have caused some legal trouble for him."

"Matt didn't tell me any of that," the chief grumbled.

My cheeks heated, and I let out an awkward laugh. I only knew the information because of a ghost. "No? Weird. Something I said must've jogged his memory."

"Must've." The grit behind the word told me that Raymond was scowling on the other end of the line. "Well, I'll look into it. Thanks, Rosie."

"Anytime," I said, hanging up the call.

Puffing out my cheeks, I nodded to Asher, and we continued on to the studio.

"Ready?" he asked.

I nodded, hoping I wasn't about to meet the man who'd stabbed Captain Westover.

14

The art studio was hard to miss. In lieu of any typical business signage, the words Joseph Fairhaven Art had been painted across the largest of the front windows in messy, dripping brushstrokes. Asher and I stepped inside. A cowbell jangled on the door handle to alert the artist to our arrival.

It was a good ten degrees hotter inside the small space, which made beads of sweat pop up along my temples almost immediately. A slightly musty smell hung in the air, along with the sharp chemical smell of cleaning solutions. The soft scent of linen sat under it all. Enormous canvases were propped up throughout the space; some were splattered haphazardly with paint, while others featured objects like buildings and bridges.

The concrete floor seemed to have just as much paint on it, like it was just another of Joseph's pieces. Afternoon sunshine filtered through the dusty windows of the studio space, laying extra patterns along the multicolored canvases.

A few folding tables sat along the edges of the space.

One held paints and brushes, while the other two worked as display tables for smaller canvases of the artist's work. A rickety ladder led up to a loft, and a short hallway led to what appeared to be a bathroom and another room.

"Coming!" a man called from the back room.

I glanced at Asher to steady myself. Moments later, a man who looked to be past middle age strode down the hallway, a bright smile on his face. He was lanky and rail thin, wearing paint-splattered cargo pants and a black, long-sleeve T-shirt. I wasn't sure how he could work in those clothes. It had to be in the nineties inside. I was in shorts and a tank top, and I was still sweating.

"Welcome. Are you here to browse or are you searching for something specific?" he asked, then held out his hand. Paint had embedded itself under each of his fingernails. "I'm Joseph Fairhaven, the artist."

I shook his hand. "Rosemary. I'm here … shopping for a gift for my sister. It's her birthday in two weeks," I said, deciding it might not be the smartest thing to ambush him with questions about Captain right away. Plus, Callie's birthday really was approaching.

His sunken cheeks seemed to plump back up, and he beamed. "That's great. What kind of art is she into?" He led me over to the display tables.

"She loves nature. Do you have anything like a landscape?" I asked, spotting a few still-life oil paintings on the table to my right.

Joseph clicked his tongue, and his eyes slid across the stacks on each table. "A couple. They're somewhere around here." He slid a few to the side. "Went through a bit of a watercolor phase last year. I think there are still a few left."

From what I could see, the man worked in as many mediums as there were available. His large pieces looked more like collages, with the mixture of paint, paper, and texture. Then there were bright oil paintings, and a small stack of vibrant watercolors.

"Ah, here they are." He picked up the watercolors and handed them over to me to peruse.

There were only three, but they were equally gorgeous. Each was a painting of the water. And while one was definitely the Columbia River, the other two were depictions of the Pacific Ocean.

One stood out. It was a churning, white-capped ocean sitting below gray, stormy clouds. A blush-colored sunset cut through it all, lighting up the painting and making the wild scene seem peaceful. It was breathtaking. The balance of blue waves, with the gray-and-white clouds, all being brought to life by the fiery yellows, oranges, and pinks of the sunset.

"I think this is the one," I said.

Joseph held it up, setting the other two aside. "I remember that day. I was down the coast a little ways to the south. A little place called Pebble Cove. It's this tiny little fishing village."

I bit back a gasp. This was our slice of the coastline. Now it was even more perfect for Callie. I was about to tell him that Pebble Cove was where I lived, but I felt a hand gently close over mine.

Asher stood next to me, his hand squeezing mine for just a moment before he let go. It was a gentle reminder. Right. The fact that Joseph knew where Pebble Cove was only added to the evidence that he could've been the one to hurt Captain. I needed to keep that to myself.

We discussed the price and he told me he'd wrap it up for me to go. Feeling like the price was way too low for the amazing piece I was getting, I fished out twice as much cash and handed it over.

Joseph's eyes went wide. "Oh, thank you. You know, I think I have a frame lying around that would work well with this piece. Let me throw that in as well." He took the cash and rifled through a stack of frames in the corner.

While he set the piece in the frame, I shoved my hands into my pockets.

"I'm glad I found you. I'm only in town today, and I had some business to take care of at the sail loft down the river." I gestured back toward Captain's warehouse.

Joseph's eyes lit up. "Cap's place?"

"Yeah, do you know him?" I asked.

At that, Joseph's shoulders slumped. "I did. He just recently died."

"Right. I heard that," I said, studying Joseph as he wrapped Callie's art piece. "Tragic."

Joseph snorted. I waited for him to follow the sound with the first unflattering opinion of the deceased man I'd heard. But he snorted again, this time grabbing a paint-stained rag from the table and swiping it under his nose. That was when I realized he was crying.

"I'm sorry." Joseph blew his nose into the rag.

Was he sad because he felt guilty? I wondered, inching back from the man.

"Hearing about what happened to him was just such a

punch to the gut. I still can't believe it. He was so great." Joseph's tearstained face angled up toward me.

I guess not.

"How well did you know him?" I asked. If Joseph wasn't the killer, maybe I could still get some information out of him.

"Only met him once." Joseph sniffed. "It's a funny story, actually." He handed over the wrapped watercolor and leaned back to sit on the edge of the display table. "My buddy let me take out his seaplane about a month ago. I had a painting I needed to get to a client in Seaside, but it was too big to fit in my car. It would've cost a small fortune to ship. I was all ready to rent a moving truck for the day when Sean told me I could just borrow his plane and fly it down."

My expression must've been the picture of surprise and doubt, because Joseph held up both his hands.

"Don't worry, I know how to fly. It might not look like it, but I grew up in a rich family. Flying lessons were a given, along with passive-aggressive family holidays." He barked out a laugh. "Anyway, I'll admit that I was a little rusty. And it showed when I was making my landing back here in Astoria. I came down too early and clipped Captain's boat with one of the floats. Luckily, the float was fine, but I couldn't say as much for Captain's boat." Joseph groaned. "I was so embarrassed, but even worse, there was no way I could've paid for the damage." He surveyed the small studio. "The life of a struggling artist, am I right?"

"What did you do?" I asked.

Joseph scratched at his elbow. "Cap said not to worry about it. He said he could pay for the repairs on his boat, no problem."

My eyes went wide. "That's so nice."

Asher paced as he listened. The space was small, though, so he walked through one of the tables with each pass.

"I know," Joseph said. "That was my reaction too. I still can't believe how generous he was. Just like I can't believe he's gone."

"So he didn't even get a lawyer involved?" I asked, remembering what Matt had said about the meeting he'd seen on Cap's schedule with the unfamiliar lawyer.

"Do I look like a guy who can afford a lawyer?" Joseph placed a hand on his chest. "No, I left that life behind when I cut ties with my family."

Then what was the lawyer for? I wondered.

Joseph must've mistaken my confusion about the lawyer for curiosity about why he'd left his family, because he added, "They weren't much of a family. It wasn't a significant loss. They never supported me. Always made me feel like I was damaged because I wanted something different than money and status."

"I'm so sorry about your family," I said. "I think it's definitely their loss. Well, we'd better get going." I checked my watch.

"We?" Joseph asked with an amused smile.

A nervous laugh bubbled out of me. "Me and this piece of art." I held up the painting.

The artist waved at me as I walked out into the warm summer evening. It probably wasn't any cooler outside, but after standing in the stuffy studio, the fresh air felt amazing. I waited until I was down the street a way to speak to Asher.

"Yet another person who loved Captain," I said, unable to keep the defeat from my tone.

It wasn't as if I wanted Joseph to be a murderer. I liked his scattered, emotional personality. And he certainly made amazing art. But the artist had been further proof that it was going to be harder than I thought to locate anyone who had a motive to kill Captain Westover.

"He sounds like he was unfailingly kind, overwhelmingly generous, and understanding beyond measure." I threw my hands in the air, careful to keep hold of Callie's painting. "Who would have any reason to kill someone like that?"

Asher arched an eyebrow. "Maybe people who don't value those same things? People who were upset with him putting empathy before profits?" he suggested.

"Like investors in his business?" I considered that. "You might be onto something. And there's still the mystery lawyer that he met with to investigate. That could be a lead."

Asher glanced down the hill toward where the sail loft sat along the river. "We can stop and ask Trip if he can get us the name."

I wrinkled my nose. "I'm sure the chief got the name of the lawyer. We can ask him when we get back to Pebble Cove." I paused, my gaze cutting over to Ash. "Plus, I want to make sure we have time to stop by the maritime museum, like Trip mentioned." I let the suggestion hang in the air between us, stopping on a street corner.

Asher's face went slack with surprise. "Oh. That sounds ... that would be ... sure." He bobbed his head in a nervous nod.

"If you want," I added. "It's just, I got the feeling back

there that you're interested in checking things out while we're here." I pushed down the sick feeling that cropped up in my stomach as I mentioned doing any more investigating into his case. The possibility that we could stumble onto the key to his case felt like a tingle along the backs of my arms, like a gut feeling.

"It makes sense to look into my family's business," Asher said. "While we're here." He made a throat-clearing noise.

An awkward air sat between us as we continued along the river walk. The smell of pitch baking in the sun mixed with the fresh breeze blowing in off the expansive river.

"We could come up with a password," Asher said after a moment.

"For what?" I wrinkled my nose in question. A seagull cawed overhead.

"If we're getting too close to something," he clarified, "either of us can say the password and we know we have to leave that second."

Either of us. Right. Really, he meant me, but I appreciated the sentiment. The reminder of the semi panic attack I'd experienced with Riley the other day proved that everything could fall into place in the blink of an eye.

"That works," I said. Just the thought of having a failsafe if I felt like things were getting out of control made my shoulders drop from where they'd been bunched up by my earlobes. "What should our password be?"

Asher squinted as he thought. "Pineapple?"

I giggled. He'd been thoroughly entranced by the fruit when I'd brought one home from the store a couple of weeks ago, admitting he'd never tasted one while he'd been alive. And even though Callie and I had explained the tropical fruit and its unique flavor to him, Asher still seemed to count it as an inexplicable mystery.

"Pineapple it is," I said.

We walked the rest of the way in silence, but Ash reached out and held my hand as we sauntered along the river walk. I didn't even care if anyone saw me holding on to thin air. It was worth it to feel whole, to experience something as normal as taking a walk with the person you loved most.

When we arrived at the museum, all the serenity I'd accumulated during our walk vanished. Banners boasting the largest collection of maritime artifacts in the country made my stomach flip. If there was information about Asher's family business, this would definitely be the place to search.

Stepping through the large glass doors, my gaze caught on a display of a Coast Guard boat scaling a fake but treacherous-looking wave. Asher stared, too, and I left him there while I went to pay the entry fee. It was crowded for a Monday evening.

When I returned to Asher's side, I resisted the urge to grab his hand again to steady mine.

We were surrounded by spirits.

And while many of the men and women walking around us appeared slightly transparent like Asher this far from home, I wondered how many of the solid-looking people were also spirits.

We were about to step forward when Asher sucked in a surprised breath. His attention had caught on a stooped older spirit. He wore tweed pants and suspenders, much like Asher. When his icy blue eyes caught on Asher, he froze.

"Lyle?" Asher asked, the name almost a growl in his throat. "Lyle Hulquist?" He squinted, like he wasn't sure what he was seeing.

My blood went cold, turning to ice right on the spot. The letter Riley had brought in on Saturday, the one he'd been so excited about, had mentioned that very name. Lyle, the man who took over managing the Benson Fishing Company after Asher was killed. The only suspect I had left in his death.

"Pineapple!" I said, my voice echoing off the vaulted ceilings of the quiet museum.

15

Every single soul in the Columbia River Maritime Museum, both living and dead, turned to look at me after my outburst. The once bustling museum fell silent.

I coughed, my neck and chest burning with embarrassment. But embarrassment had nothing on the other emotion I was experiencing: fear.

I needed to get Asher out of the museum and away from Lyle Hulquist: the man who had, quite possibly, killed him.

Asher's attention flicked between me and the alarmed-looking Lyle. I grabbed for Asher's arm, but without him pushing energy into it, my fingers just wafted right through him.

"We need to leave. Pineapple. I repeat. Pineapple," I said through gritted teeth, painfully aware of the eyes still on me as I swatted at thin air.

Irises shifting to a dark, stormy blue, Asher finally focused on me. "Rosemary, what's—?" His question ended abruptly. He didn't need to finish because he'd answered it himself.

My pulse pounded in my ears, my whole body flushed with worry, and tears pricked at the corners of my eyes. I couldn't lose him yet. "Ash, please. We said no questions. We have to leave."

Full understanding settled over him. He knew. Lyle was his killer. My gaze flashed over to the man who was staring at my best friend like he was a plague on this earth. The hateful glare Lyle fixed us with told me he would kill Asher all over again if he could.

Asher followed me as I scampered out of the museum, still attracting the attention of most of the guests and staff members until I was safely outside. I wouldn't have blamed them if they'd felt the need to lock the doors behind me.

Once we were outside, I kept up a quick pace, as if the more space there was between us and the museum, the safer we were. Asher's face was contorted into a grimace. His eyes shifted back and forth, looking at nothing in particular as he walked, like he was flicking through old memory clips. He blinked rapidly as he seemed to put it all together.

Suddenly a fresh fear took hold of my throat, tightening down like a vise. I came to an abrupt stop.

Asher had figured it out. Was I too late? Would I lose him anyway?

"Ash," I whispered to his retreating form. He hadn't realized I'd stopped, caught up in his own thoughts.

But my tiny voice reached him. He turned back toward me. His face softened, losing all its hard lines and anger in an instant.

"Oh, Rosie," he breathed out my name as he moved back toward me, wrapping me up into a tight hug.

Yes, there were other people milling about on the sidewalk who probably thought I was crazy, hugging the air like I was while clutching a wrapped piece of art. But when you're not sure if your best friend, the soul you love, is about to leave you forever—and you just yelled "pineapple" in a crowded museum—you don't care so much about looking like you're out of your mind.

Asher stepped back, unable to hold me tight for very long this far from home, even with the jasper stones he carried. It was an aching reminder of his limitations as a spirit.

I swallowed, unable to force out the questions I needed to ask. *Do you feel different? Is it happening? Are you moving on?*

Asher's eyes searched mine, and he seemed to understand. "No," he said softly. "I'm okay. I don't think this is it. First, I don't know how Lyle could've killed me." He snorted. "Though I have a few guesses why."

Relief washed through me like a gulp of ice water after a week in the desert. I followed Asher as he walked along the river, back toward the marina. We didn't technically have to leave for the boat just yet, but it seemed smart to head back in that direction. The evening air was warm, and the smell of baking dough wafted over to us as we passed by a pizzeria.

Asher peered over at me. "When did you learn about Lyle?"

"A few days ago," I croaked out the confession. "Catherine mentioned him in one of her letters to your sister."

"You don't have to tell me, but do you know all of it?" he asked.

My heart sank. He thought I was keeping the details

from him. He thought I already had all the answers. I couldn't blame him. I'd kept many secrets from him before, especially when I thought it would protect him. And I couldn't promise that if I learned the details behind his death, that I wouldn't hold on to them until I was ready.

But that wasn't the case here. I shook my head emphatically. "No, just an inkling. I know about as much as you do." I squinted. "At least I think I do. Did he really hate you because you liked to read?"

Asher let out a derisive laugh. "I mean, that was the root of the problem. But no. He hated that I was his boss just because of the family I'd been born into. It didn't help that I wasn't interested in the business or that I preferred to read in my spare time." Asher looked momentarily worried. "Don't get me wrong. I was actually not bad at the business part of the company. I didn't slack off. But learning all the ins and outs about the boats? That's the stuff I didn't care about. And that's what Lyle lived for."

"So he complained that he could do a better job running the company than you?" I asked, worried I might be too close to the actual motive for murder.

Asher scoffed. "Made a point to tell me every day." The river rushed by as we walked. "I just wish he had known that I never planned to stay," Asher said.

He'd mentioned all of this before: his father's disappointment that he didn't want to follow in his footsteps, the way he saw Asher's time at university studying English as a waste, and how Asher had joined the army as a way to garner respect from his father.

"I stepped in after I graduated, knowing I was leaving for war, and I'd fully planned on telling Archie that I couldn't continue once I got back." Asher sighed. "*If* I got back. Which I didn't … just for different reasons."

"It seems weird that Lyle wouldn't have just waited until after the war," I said, bringing up the same question I'd mentioned to Riley. "I mean, you very well *could've* died. Why become a murderer if he didn't have to?"

"It is odd." Asher dipped his chin. "I can only guess that it had more to do with his hatred of me, and getting me out of the way so he could run the company was just a perk?" Asher guessed. He glanced over his shoulder, back toward the museum.

"Well, I guess we know where to get the answers to that … when we're ready," I said.

Asher locked eyes with me, holding me in such a tight embrace without even touching me that I stopped walking to look up at him. "When we're ready," he repeated.

But the sadness behind his blue eyes, and the pain that flinched through his face in tremors, gave away his true feelings. He didn't need to hide them. They were my feelings too.

"I don't think I'll ever be ready," I whispered, my words breaking as a tear streamed down my cheeks.

Ash reached forward and cupped my cheek, swiping away the tear. He said nothing, as if he couldn't trust himself to speak. Asher let his hand drop back by his side, and it went transparent yet again. We kept walking.

"Do you ever wonder …?" I started but chewed on my lip as I thought through the emotions I was experiencing. I wasn't sure what I was trying to ask.

"Often." Asher smirked playfully. "Sometimes even on purpose."

I chuckled. "Come on. I'm trying to be serious here. It's just … I feel like I was meant to meet you, Asher." Another tear clung to the corner of my eye. I blinked it away.

"Me too, Rosie."

We walked the rest of the way to the docks in silence.

———

THE TRIP back to Pebble Cove was much less eventful. The bar crossing was easier on the way home, and I didn't even get seasick. Ash and I sat together on the bow of the boat, watching the scenery pass by. It was much more crowded on the way back with the crab pots, and the crew dropped them into the water in designated areas as we puttered down the coast.

After a tough day, my heart soared when we pulled into Pebble Cove. I'd only been gone a handful of hours, but I missed my home. Well, one of my homes.

If I was being completely honest with myself, Asher was home to me more than any physical place could ever be. His soul brought out the best in mine. He'd helped me become the person I'd always wanted to be. But if I couldn't always have him around, I was glad I had people and places I loved almost as much.

Asher and I separated at the marina once we disembarked the fishing vessel. He wanted to tell the other ghosts about what we'd learned in Astoria about Captain's case, and I wanted to speak with the chief.

I crossed the street and peered through the darkness into the police station windows. There was still a light on inside. The door swung open when I tugged on it. Fischer's front desk was empty, but I rang the bell on the counter, and the chief came out from the back hallway. His eyes were ringed with dark circles and his hair mussed from his fingers raking through it.

"You're back." He cocked an eyebrow at me.

"I have information to share," I said.

He glanced at the wrapped artwork I clutched.

I moved it behind my back. "Not this. That's for Callie's birthday."

He snapped his fingers. "Thanks for the reminder." He stared at the ceiling for a moment like he was making a mental note. "I'm still getting the hang of this dad thing." He picked at a thread on his uniform.

My heart warmed. "You're doing a great job."

"Come have a seat." He waved me back to his office.

Pressing my lips together so I wouldn't grin like an idiot about this change in my new father, I followed him. In a couple of years, he'd gone from thinking I was involved in every crime that happened in town to asking for my help in solving them.

We walked past the holding cell, and I noticed the Rickster was still inside. I wondered when I'd need to go check on his animals again.

"So what'd you learn?" the chief asked as we settled into chairs on either side of his desk. "I'm guessing it has something to do with the artist, Joseph Fairhaven." He glanced meaningfully at the piece of art as I set it in the empty chair next to me.

My mouth fell open. "You checked up on him?" I hadn't told Raymond anything but Joseph's name. He would've had to look him up to find out he was an artist.

"Of course," he scoffed. "I knew you would go find him after we talked, so I wanted to make sure you weren't walking into a dangerous situation." Raymond shrugged. "He doesn't have a record and seems harmless enough."

"That's what I found as well," I said. "The seaplane incident was entirely his fault, and he said Captain was gracious and kind about the accident. He paid for it all, letting Joseph completely off the hook."

Raymond's eyebrows elevated. "The more I learn about this man, the more of a saint he seems to be." He ran his palm along the stubble on his chin. "I can't help but wonder if it's all true."

"Me too." I pulled in a long inhale. "Oh, but Matt mentioned Captain talking to a lawyer who differed from the normal one he kept on retainer. At first, I thought it could've been connected to the seaplane incident, like someone was trying to sue him, but Joseph said they kept insurance and lawyers out of it. So this lawyer could be our clue to something else. You didn't get a name for the lawyer he met with about a month ago, did you?"

The chief flipped open his notes. "I did, actually. His name is Anthony Farrow. I've checked into him. He's an intellectual-property lawyer. I've got a call in to his secretary, but apparently he's out on vacation for the rest of the week, and he'll call me back when he can." Raymond rolled his eyes. "What's even more interesting was what I found out from Fallon Bergstrom, the lawyer Captain kept on retainer."

I leaned forward.

"Cap recently bought up a large piece of land," Raymond said. "Well, he was in the process. He was supposed to sign the papers today, but he never made it to that deal."

"You think someone killed him to stop him from buying the land?" I asked.

The chief tapped the tip of his nose. "The acreage is just to the east of us, in the valley. It's currently owned by a family who's lived there for almost a century. Fallon said she didn't know what Cap was going to use it for, but he'd instructed her to make sure the land contract was airtight."

I gasped. "Maybe the family didn't want to sell, and he was pressuring them."

"My exact thought." Raymond's eyes sparkled. "I'm going to go talk to the family tomorrow, if you want to tag along."

I blinked. "You want *me* to come with?" I couldn't hide the shock from my voice if I'd tried.

He cleared his throat. "To be honest, Officer Gerard was the one who recommended that I bring you instead of one of them. She grew up on a farm and said they might respond better if they feel like they can trust me, that I'm on their side. Bringing one of my daughters with might help soften me in their eyes."

That sounded more like it. But I didn't care what the reason was. I was about to say yes when the bell on Fischer's desk rang. The chief and I regarded each other, confusion evident in our wrinkled foreheads.

"Helloooo," a woman's voice trilled out from the front foyer.

We got up to go see who it was.

The Rickster called out to me on my way past his cell. "Hey, wait."

I hung back, letting the chief walk ahead.

The Rickster's eyes were wide. "Hide me," he pleaded. "Tell her I'm not here." He examined the space like he was checking for a hidden exit. "Tell her I'm dead. I got stabbed too."

"Is this the assassin?" I asked, mostly joking.

His face paled. "Worse. It's my ex-wife."

16

———

"Your ex-wife? One of the Hollywood actresses?" I asked the Rickster with a smirk as we waited.

Talk around town, no doubt started by the Rickster himself, was that he'd been married to not one, but two Hollywood actresses.

To my surprise, however, the Rickster nodded gravely. "And this is the successful one." He shivered.

Before he could say anything more, Chief Clemenson entered the room, followed closely behind by a woman who could've stepped right off a Broadway stage before showing up in Pebble Cove.

She was in her seventies, like the Rickster, but had aged as gracefully as she walked—the woman sauntered like she was on a catwalk. She wore a long silk scarf over a simple black dress. The purples and greens in the scarf complemented her gray hair, which was swept up into a chignon.

"Richard," the woman said, stopping short once she caught sight of the Rickster in his holding cell.

She said his name in a biting way, like he was the king in

the Shakespeare play and she was about to run him through with a sword or two.

I almost expected him to call out, asking someone to fetch him a horse.

Instead, his face broke into a boyish grin. "Celeste, come to try to make me fall in love with you again?" He waggled his eyebrows at the woman.

The change in tone surprised me so much that my mouth dropped open. Hadn't he just compared her to an assassin?

Celeste cocked an eyebrow, unamused. But then her lips twitched into a reluctant smile, and she said, "We both know you never stopped loving me, Richard."

My jaw officially dropped. The chief was just as confused by the interaction. He and I stood there glancing between these two characters like we were watching some sort of soap opera unfold before our eyes.

"I thought you hated her?" The question flew from my mouth before I could hold it in.

The Rickster chuckled. "We have a bit of a love-hate thing going."

"Meaning, he hates how much he still loves me." Celeste smirked in my direction.

"How'd you know I was here, kitten?" the Rickster propped an arm on the bars of his holding cell.

Kitten? I coughed to hide my surprise.

"A little birdie told me," she said.

I wondered if that meant Celeste had spies in Pebble Cove, but then the Rickster said, "How *is* our boy?"

Boy? Did the Rickster have a son?

"You should call him more than to tell him you're in jail

and 'it's not looking good.'" Celeste's tone flattened as she repeated what the Rickster had most likely said.

"I wanted to let him know, just in case." The Rickster shrugged.

She clicked her tongue. "He's worried about you."

"So he sent *you*?" The Rickster barked out a laugh. "You get me into more trouble than I could ever get into on my own."

The chief and I simultaneously raised our eyebrows. We both knew how much trouble the Rickster could get in on his own.

Celeste whirled toward me and the chief. "I demand he be let out on bail. I will pay whatever fees are necessary." She pushed her chin up in the air like she was punctuating the end of a scene.

The chief rubbed his hand over the back of his neck. "He's free to go. We haven't charged him yet. It's his choice to stay here."

Turning her attention back to her ex-husband, Celeste didn't even need to speak. Her scowl said it all.

The Rickster put up both his hands, as if she were a police officer and he'd been caught red-handed … again. "It's safer in here, my love. I have an assassin after me. They killed Cap." On those last words, his voice broke.

Celeste's perfect posture slumped, her shoulders folding forward. "Johnathan told me. I'm devastated." It wasn't until she said those words, broken and real, that I realized all of her other sentences had sounded like practiced lines from a play. But the emotion that showed when she talked about Captain was honest.

As though she'd only forgotten her lines for a moment,

she straightened up and said, "Don't worry about assassins. I'm here now. You're safer with me than in this cell."

Somehow, I didn't doubt it. Celeste was a force of nature.

The chief checked with the Rickster, who moved to stand next to the metal door. Raymond unlocked the holding cell and held a hand out, showing the Rickster he was free to go. He stepped forward, saluting the chief and sending me a discreet wink. I reminded myself to talk to him about telling people he'd hired me—unless he actually wanted to pay me—but I figured it could wait. I didn't want to bring it up in front of Celeste. They had enough to discuss.

"Trickster and Atticus will be thrilled to have a guest," the Rickster said.

Celeste scoffed, "I'm not staying on that moldy little houseboat of yours. We're getting a room at The Gull's Nest. I will settle for nothing less than a king-sized bed and a soaking tub." She flicked her scarf over one shoulder and led the way out of the station.

The Rickster followed like, well, kind of like Atticus, his pet duck, often followed at his heels. And then they were gone.

"That was something else," I said, widening my eyes at Raymond.

He let out a low whistle, then clapped his hands together as if removing dust. "Well, with him gone, I can head home for the night."

I smiled. "Say hi to Mom for me."

"I will." He turned back toward his office but snapped his fingers and pivoted back to face me. "She wants you girls to come over on Saturday for dinner, if that works for you."

"That should work. I'll check with Callie and let you know." Waving goodbye, I walked back to my car. It had been a long day, and I was excited to get back home.

The teahouse windows glowed with a warm yellow light when I pulled up a few minutes later. I know I'd been on the water most of the day, but there was something different about the crashing waves along my beach. My heart ached as I glanced out toward the surf, doing my usual check for Asher. He had a propensity for standing at the water's edge and getting lost as he stared at the waves undulating and curling toward the shore.

He wasn't anywhere to be seen in the deepening dark, so I headed inside.

Normally, the bitter scent of tea was punctuated with the sugary treats Callie baked up each day to serve in the tea shop. It created a cozy atmosphere that made me want to wrap my fingers around a mug and lose myself in a book.

As I stepped into the front hallway, there *was* a bitter smell, all right, but this wasn't the earthy scent of tea leaves. The acrid scent of charred food sat heavy in the house. A layer of smoke undulated in the air as the door shut behind me.

"Callie?" I asked, panic raising the pitch of my voice as I called out her name.

Pots and pans slammed together in the kitchen. Stashing her art in the hallway closet, I ran toward the sounds. Fears and worries scrambled after me. Was she in trouble? Was the house on fire? Could she not even stop to yell out a hello because she was currently battling the flames?

The smoke thickened as I approached our small kitchen, and Callie coughed.

"Cal, you in here?" I waved my hand in front of my face as I stepped into the kitchen to clear some of the smoke.

The window next to the sink cracked open and fresh air poured into the room at the same time that it sucked the smoky air out. Callie hunched over the sink, her hands pressing down onto the countertop, like she was having a small breakdown. A pan of unrecognizably burnt food sat atop the stove.

"Holy smokes," I said, then giggled. "Do our smoke detectors not work?" I calmed down now that I could see she was okay and only the food had burned, not the house.

"Oh, they work. I took them down after I burned the first batch." Callie didn't turn around as she spoke. Her tone was flat, but there was a quiet rage underneath, threatening to disturb her calm façade.

The simmering anger evident in her taut posture wasn't like Callie. She was usually so easygoing and happy.

"What were you trying to make?" I asked, eyeing the charred remains of food.

Her back lifted and dropped with a heavy sigh. "Those were supposed to be quiches. I already ruined a batch of bread pudding by using salt instead of sugar. I wanted to try out a few new dishes while you were gone, but it turned out to be a terrible idea."

"Why wait until I was gone?" I frowned, not understanding. I'd acted as her sous-chef many a time.

At that, Callie spun around, and her eyes met mine. Hers were narrowed in frustration. "Because I didn't want to bother you. I didn't want to monopolize the kitchen and make you try things you might not like." She gestured wildly as she spoke.

"Bother me?" was all I could eke out before breaking into a coughing fit.

I wasn't much of a cook, so I was almost never in the kitchen. And even if I had been, she would never have been in my way. And what was this about food I didn't like? The list of things I wouldn't try was relatively short, I thought.

Callie stood there, her jaw clenched and fists balled together, tight.

"Cal, I know I've been distracted lately." I stepped forward, a hand raised in what I hoped would be a white flag of surrender. "I'm really sorry if I've made you feel like I'm not here for you." Perking up at the memory of the art, I realized this might be the perfect way to lift her mood. "Hold on a sec." I lifted one finger, rushing back to the hallway closet where I'd stashed the painting.

The kitchen had mostly cleared of smoke when I returned.

"How do you feel about an early birthday present?" I asked. "I know it's still a couple of weeks away, but … well, here." I pushed the wrapped piece of art forward.

Callie pursed her lips and then reached for the present. She unwrapped it carefully, like it might contain jumping spiders. When the paper peeled back enough for her to see what was inside, she inhaled softly.

"It's our beach." I beamed.

Tears rushed to her eyes, creating a glassy look that matched the watercolor surface of the ocean in the painting. "Rosemary, I—" She rushed toward me, pulling me into a tight hug. "Is it okay if I clean all of this up in the morning?

I think I'm going to go to bed early," she said, her words muffled by my hair as I wrapped my arms around her and squeezed back.

"Sure," I said, still completely in the dark about what was going on.

"Good night." She took her painting with her and padded into the tearoom, her footsteps creaking up the old staircase before her bedroom door clicked shut.

I was about halfway through cleaning the kitchen—as quietly as I could—when Asher appeared next to me.

"Whoa. What happened here?" He took a surprised step back as he surveyed the damage.

I wrinkled my nose. "I don't know. When I got home, Callie had burned a bunch of food and she was fuming mad. I've never seen her like this, Ash." I chewed on my lip as I looked at him.

He curled his lip at the charred remains I'd discarded into the garbage can. "I'd say something's definitely wrong."

I nodded. It looked like I had one more mystery to add to the list of cases that needed to be solved around here, and by the state of our kitchen, I needed to sort this out fast.

17

The next morning, I woke to the usual sounds of Callie up early, baking for the shop. I crossed my fingers that the clean kitchen she'd woken up to had improved her mood instead of adding to the anger she seemed to be experiencing.

Before I could even make it out of bed, my phone buzzed with a text. It was from Raymond.

Leaving for the valley in about twenty minutes. Want me to swing by and pick you up?

Another clatter arose from the kitchen, and I winced.

As much as I wanted to go with the chief and investigate the land deal Captain had been working on when he'd died, I couldn't leave Callie here alone today. After seeing her so distraught last night, I needed to be here for her today.

With a deep sigh, I sent a response.

I'm so sorry to bail, but I think Callie needs me here at the shop today. Can you bring Fischer instead?

Any guilt I felt at taking away the chief's upper hand by

bringing his adopted daughter along for questioning flitted away when he sent another text moments later.

Don't be sorry. You're a good friend and sister. Talk soon.

His text gave me hope he would still share whatever he found in the valley. I crossed my fingers that I'd made the right decision.

Padding carefully downstairs, I kept my fingers crossed as I walked warily into the kitchen. The scent of cinnamon swirled through the air. Based on the perfectly golden brown tiny quiches cooling on the rack and the cinnamon toast smell, Callie had successfully completed both of the recipes she'd failed at creating last night.

"Morning," I said.

But even though these batches were perfect, Callie's eyes were still red with tears as she turned around. Immediately, I knew I'd made the right choice to stay. I suddenly wished Asher was here to help me navigate this situation, but he was watching over the Rickster to make sure no more assassination attempts happened. Despite Celeste's confidence that she'd be enough of a deterrent, Asher hadn't wanted to take any chances, so he was keeping an eye out for them.

"Hi, Rosemary." Callie sniffed. "Thank you for cleaning. I'm so sorry about last night." Her voice wobbled like she might break into sobs at any moment. Based on her puffy eyes, it had already happened at least once this morning.

"It's okay," I said, my shoulders dropping in relief. "Do you want to talk about what's been going on?"

Callie swallowed hard. "What do you mean? Nothing's going on."

I tilted my head to one side. "Cal," was all I had to say for her to close her eyes and exhale.

"Fine," she said. "I'm not doing well."

"Does this have to do with what you and Owen were fighting about the other day?" I asked.

She nodded. "I've been having a hard time feeling like I have a place around here." She flapped a tea towel toward the tearoom. "He wanted me to talk to you and Jolene, but I wasn't ready yet."

It took me a moment to absorb her words. Even after I did, I blinked as I struggled to understand them. Wait. This didn't have to do with Owen? They'd only been fighting because he was trying to get her to tell *me* the truth. I was the problem.

Confusion wrapped itself around me as I tried to take her words to heart. She didn't have a place? But she'd fit in here from the moment she set foot in this house after washing up on the beach with amnesia. In fact, she'd fit in so well that she'd left the life she thought she wanted in Portland to stay here in Pebble Cove.

"Of course you have a place." I stepped forward.

But Callie raised a hand to keep me at bay. "Rosie, just listen. I'm not saying you and Jolene haven't been amazing and welcoming. I've absolutely loved working with the two of you in this business, but it's *your* business."

"We could talk about adding you as a third partner," I said quickly, wondering why I hadn't thought about it before. We paid Callie well, but I could understand if she wanted to be an equal partner.

Callie shook her head. "It's your business with Jolene. And it makes sense. Both of you have a place. You make the

tea and Jo makes the baked items. You two work together."
She cocked an eyebrow. "Though, if you ask me, you need
to decide on one name so customers who aren't from
around here stop assuming the two of you are in
competition."

She was right. We'd been putting it off. But I couldn't
think about renaming the shop now. I had more important
matters to deal with.

"Let's set up a meeting, then. Just the three of us. We
can discuss how to help you find what you want to do." I
chewed on my lip hopefully as I watched my friend.

"The thing is … I've found what I want to do," she said,
bowing her head forward in shame.

"That's great." I couldn't help but choke out a laugh.
"Then why do you look so miserable?"

Tears crowded Callie's eyes. "Because I love how things
are and I don't want them to change." I was about to tell her
that nothing needed to change, when she quickly added,
"But I also really want to try out this new thing. I'm just
scared."

Stepping forward and placing a gentle hand on Callie's
arm, I asked, "What is it?" Worry engulfed me. Would this
new endeavor take my other best friend away? Losing Asher
was going to be hard enough. I wasn't sure if I could go
through this all without my sister too.

Her watery eyes flashed up to meet mine. "Georgie and
Sam offered me The Gull's Nest bed-and-breakfast," she
blurted out as if she knew she would chicken out if she
paused for even a second.

My tight posture loosened at the news. "What? That's
amazing."

Callie's lips pulled into a tentative smile. "I mean, they want me to manage it with them for a few years. But they're getting closer to retirement age, and Sam's knees aren't fit for going up and down those stairs multiple times each day. They originally thought about asking Owen, but he loves what he's doing on the police force and doing both jobs would be too much. So when we started getting serious, they came up with the idea that it could be me."

Suddenly the specific foods that were in our kitchen made sense. The Gull's Nest was locally famous for Georgie's bread pudding, served to guests as dessert upon request. And Sam's mini quiches made the perfect breakfast.

"I was trying to come up with my own version of their classic recipes last night, but my nerves got the best of me," Callie explained, seeing that I'd put the pieces together. "I was worried you'd come home early and catch me and then know why I was baking those particular items and—" She stopped, running out of steam all at once.

"Oh, Callie." I pulled her into a hug. "I'm ecstatic for you." I stepped back, holding her at arm's length and fixing her with a stern look. "As long as it's what you want. All I want is for you to be happy."

She nodded emphatically. "It is. I think it will make me happy. At first, I was a little worried about getting involved in business with Owen's family. I mean, I don't *think* we'll break up, but what if something changes? Still, I think I'd be more upset with myself if I didn't at least try. The minute Georgie brought it up to me and Owen, my mind started spinning with ideas. It felt like when I first started baking, I couldn't stop thinking up new recipes and trying out new ideas."

I remembered that time period. Callie had been joyous in her recipe testing. It seemed like she would try something new each day. Lately, however, she'd just been sticking to our usual fare, recreating Jolene's staples instead of innovating any of her own.

"I think this is going to be perfect," I said, my heart finally relaxing now that I knew the truth about what was bothering my friend.

Callie's grin fell. "But it's going to mean that I live there, at the bed-and-breakfast." Tears gathered in her eyes again. "I'm not going to live with you anymore." Now she was full-on crying.

I felt my own eyes welling up with tears at the thought. Of course she would have to move into The Gull's Nest. She would need to live on-site to help with day-to-day operations and be there for the guests, as well as supporting Georgie and Sam.

My mouth formed a small o. "Right." I shook my head. "It'll be fine. I'll miss you so much, but we'll still see each other a ton. It's not like you're moving to a different town." I waved a dismissive hand toward her.

Callie's eyes held mine. They narrowed seriously. "Rosemary, I'm worried about you being here all alone."

I scoffed. "I won't be here alone. I've got Ash—"

And that's when it hit me. I wouldn't have him for much longer.

We knew who'd killed Asher. We'd finally figured it out. All that we had to do was make the trip up to Astoria again and confront Lyle's ghost in the maritime museum to learn the truth behind the why and how, and Asher would be gone forever. We were just biding our time, just waiting until we could say our last goodbyes.

And then I really would be alone.

I sucked in a quick breath, like someone had stabbed me in the gut. But I quickly shook away the feeling, knowing Callie was already worried about me. I didn't want to make that worse. I didn't want to be the reason that she didn't follow her dreams.

Callie's timer went off, snapping us out of our emotional state. She sent me an apologetic look before moving to the timer to quiet it and donning her oven mitts. A rush of warm cinnamon-scented air whirled through the room as she opened the oven. The scent only intensified as she pulled out the tray of perfectly browned, amazing-smelling bread pudding.

The cinnamon was a bit of a punch to the gut, however, because that had been the base to the blend I'd made up to honor Asher the other day, and ever since he'd asked me to use that spice, I'd been associating the scent with him.

Callie turned off the oven and swiveled to face me once more. She puffed out her cheeks.

"Hey," I said, reaching forward to grab ahold of her hand. "I'd be lying if I said it won't be hard without the two of you here with me. But it's how it needs to be. Hard or not, we'll figure everything out." I checked my watch. "We've got to open this tea shop. Okay?"

"Okay," Callie said, with a nod that looked about as unconvinced as I felt.

There was no way to sugarcoat it. Things were going to change, and it was going to be hard. We just had to believe we could get through it all unscathed.

———

THE SHOP WAS HOPPING for a Tuesday. The chess club met as usual, but they seemed to have doubled in size. Callie blamed it on a new chess-themed movie that had just come out, renewing people's interest in the timeless game. The busy state of the shop helped to distract us from the difficult conversation we'd had in the kitchen that morning.

Well, until Daphne.

"Wait. Quiches and bread pudding?" my neighbor asked suspiciously when she clomped in an hour after we opened. Her eyes swiveled between the two baked items. "What's going on here? Why are you serving staples from The Gull's Nest?" Daphne narrowed her eyes, then she gasped. "You're going to take over for Georgie and Sam, aren't you?" she screeched out the question as she pointed to Callie.

The whole tea shop went quiet as everyone inside turned their attention to Callie and waited for her response.

Callie's cheeks turned a violent shade of pink. Her shoulders scrunched up near her ears in a sign of intense discomfort. "I ... uh ... yeah?" She practically whispered it.

Daphne clapped once in triumph. "I knew it!" Then, getting over the initial high of being right, she patted Callie's hand. "Congratulations, dear. You'll be great. We'll all be excited to have someone who can scale those stairs and can actually see the computer screen on that registration desk."

With that, Daphne twirled around. Not a hair on her overly coiffed head moved. She clomped out of the tea shop, her signature clogs looking even sillier when paired with coral-colored shorts she wore in preparation for the high summer temperatures we were supposed to reach today.

Customers came over and congratulated Callie over the next few hours, showing that the word had even spread downtown.

"I hope you've already told Georgie and Sam that you accepted," I muttered when we were alone behind the tea bar. "Because I think it's gotten out."

She laughed. "Yeah, they know." At that, she cringed in apology.

"I forbid you from making that face at me anymore," I said, scolding her. "I'm fine."

My words appeased Callie, but I couldn't help but feel the very definite "for now" that silently clung to the end of my sentence.

To distract myself from thinking too much about that, I turned my thoughts to Raymond, wondering what he'd found in the valley today during his investigation. I hoped it was something good, something that would break this case wide open.

After today, I needed some good news.

18

The tea shop was abuzz with excitement about Callie's impending move. In an effort to save her from the onslaught of questions, I sent her upstairs. She had packing to do, and I could see the constant reminders of how much people expected of her in this new role were getting to her.

Just when the customers settled down, the object of their gossip no longer around, the Rickster and Celeste sauntered in, hand in hand. The atmosphere turned positively giddy with excitement.

I brightened even more when Asher appeared, his watch ongoing. And even though I couldn't stop to chat with him about what had happened so far that morning, I felt better just having him around. He settled at an empty table, eyes poring over an open newspaper, when they weren't watching over the Rickster.

Celeste wore a flowing kaftan. Each time someone complimented her on it, she would just swish the flowing fabric around her legs and say, "Kaftans are the clothing of the future, my darling."

With huge sunglasses perched atop her head and hand gestures as graceful as a ballerina's, she regaled the locals with stories of her time on Broadway and her switch from stage to motion pictures. But what everyone *really* ate up were her stories about the Rickster. More specifically, it became a game to ask her to debunk the many tall tales the Rickster had told us over his time in Pebble Cove.

"This one has good luck when it comes to sharks." Celeste smiled fondly over at the Rickster. She'd just finished telling a story about his brief stint in professional poker tournaments.

"Sharks?" one fisherman asked. "So his story about the great white was true?"

Celeste lifted her chin. "Of course it's true. He could've reached out and touched that beast."

"How do you know?" someone else challenged.

Celeste crossed her arms over her chest and said, "I watched the whole thing from the shore. I was on that trip with him and Captain."

Gasps sounded around the room. And the floodgates opened. That was how it began.

"Wait, did he really get struck by lightning seven times?" someone asked.

Celeste snorted. "Seven?"

"That's what he told us," someone else whined, sounding a lot like they were tattling to parents about a sibling's behavior.

She gave a scolding look to the man sitting next to her. "Three is enough, darling. Why do you feel the need to stretch it to seven?"

The Rickster glanced sheepishly down at his hands in his lap.

"Three times? That's still a lot," someone muttered.

"Tell me about it," Celeste said. "How else do you think he gets his hair to stand up straight like that?" she asked with a chuckle, gesturing to the Rickster's signature wild white hair. She stage-whispered, "And I think it's part of the reason his brain works the way it does." She made a circle by her temple, signaling his wacky thought process. "Well, that and your insistence on climbing Everest without oxygen."

"That's true too?" A local man sat back in his chair, like he couldn't believe it.

Celeste stood by the fireplace, as if it were a makeshift stage, and she answered all the questions they could throw at her. The Rickster sat by her side, beaming up at her, and interjecting where he could.

"So he really was married to two Hollywood actresses?" another local asked.

At this, Celeste vehemently shook her head. "That is absolutely false."

The Rickster took her hand and said, "Now, now, kitten. Just because you didn't think she was a *talented* actress doesn't mean you can say she wasn't one."

To our surprise, Celeste tipped her head to one side in concession. "Fine. I *suppose* you could've called her an actress. Though she was only ever in *one* movie and a handful of stage productions, and never in the lead role." She fluffed her hair like even talking about the other woman in the Rickster's life was beneath her.

"And once I met you, I forgot everything about her," he said, planting a kiss on Celeste's hand.

Her eyes shone as she smiled down at him. Their relationship was a confusing whiplash of boiling hot and freezing cold. They loved each other one moment, only to talk about how much they despised the other in the next breath.

"Why'd the two of you split up?" The question came from Daphne. She'd somehow slipped back inside, probably after hearing that the Rickster and his famous ex-wife were in the shop.

All eyes turned to her, and the cheerful atmosphere in the place flattened.

"Daphne, it's none of our business," Carl, my other neighbor, grumbled from where he read the newspaper at the tea bar, his back to this whole discussion.

Daphne placed a hand on her chest. "What? I'm just curious. The two of you seem so in love."

When they aren't at each other's throats, I thought with an inward snicker.

Callie came down the stairs, joining me behind the tea bar. "Why's everyone staring daggers at Daphne?" she whispered.

"Because she just asked a very personal question," Carl answered for me.

Daphne blushed and huffed like she was about to give some sort of excuse and stomp off.

But Celeste spoke up before she could. "It's all right We don't mind admitting that while we are crazy about each other, we also drive each other crazy." She settled into the seat next to him. This was their story to tell together. She wasn't the leading lady anymore.

"We wanted different things out of life," the Rickster said. "Took us a long time to figure that out, but it's for the better now that we did."

Celeste scoffed. "He quit his business for me. I quit acting for a while for him. Heck, we tried it all. We're just better friends." She winked at him, making me wonder if their definition of friends was different from most people's.

As they regaled the locals with the story of how they met, the chief entered, his eight-point cap in his hands. Eyes lighting up, I walked over to him.

"How'd it go?" I asked, anticipation leaking from my excited words.

The chief motioned to the empty deck. Normally on a hot day like today, the sunny deck would've been packed with customers sipping iced tea and chatting over the sounds of the breaking waves, but with the Rickster and Celeste inside, the deck was empty. Making eye contact with Callie, I jerked my head toward the porch in question. She gave me a thumbs-up, showing me she was happy to look after the place while I talked to the chief.

Asher glanced my way, but I could see he was taking his job watching for any assassination attempts seriously, and he didn't want to leave his marks untended.

On my way outside, I grabbed two glasses and a pitcher of iced tea from the bar and brought it outside with us. I poured the chief a glass first, handing it over as he sank into one of the patio chairs.

The sea was glassy and calm today, the normal gusty breeze almost nonexistent. It made the high temperature even more intense. The only tradeoff was that without the blustery wind, I could open an umbrella to offer us some shade from the summer sunshine.

"So?" I asked, my tea untouched as I waited for him to spill about his day in the valley.

He pulled in a breath and shook his head as he exhaled. "Another dead end."

My rigid body deflated forward. "Man," I said, "I was really hoping you'd find a family willing to do whatever they could to save the ancestral lands that an evil millionaire was forcing them to sell."

The chief shook his head again. "Quite the opposite, actually. They were delighted to be selling. The farmhouse is falling apart, none of the children are interested in farming the land anymore, and Captain was offering them way more than the land was worth."

Yet another instance where he was the hero, I realized.

"Great," I said sarcastically. "Any chance it was someone outside the family? Could the locals be mad about him developing the property and putting in an enormous ware-house or something? They could've tried to get him out of the way, so that didn't happen."

The chief nodded to humor me, but said, "Another no. I saw the blueprints. He was planning on building a commu-nity center. He grew up in that town, apparently, and wanted to give back. Everyone was beyond excited about the center and the jobs it would bring to their community. They all loved him." The chief pulled out an almost empty travel pack of tissues from his pocket. "In fact, more often than not, they broke into tears the moment I mentioned Captain Westover."

Acceptance washed over me. "So it wasn't the land deal

that killed him. Which means we're back at square one, with no suspects other than the Rickster." I gestured to the roomful of locals. "Who's most likely telling the truth about what happened to Captain because Celeste is in there confirming all the crazy stuff he's told us over the years. I don't think most of what he says is actually a lie."

The chief tapped his foot under the table, like he was considering something. "We may not be *all* the way back at square one," he said. The reluctance with which he said the words told me that this was probably a large clue, and he was fighting with himself about whether to share it with me. "I talked with Fallon Bergstrom today on my drive back to Pebble Cove."

My interest piqued at the mention of Captain's lawyer. "Did she know anything about the IP lawyer he talked to or why?"

The chief shook his head. "And she sounded a little offended that he'd gone behind her back, but she admitted that intellectual property isn't her area of expertise." He stretched his shoulders back, trying to get back on track. "Anyway, that's not the most interesting thing she shared with me."

I leaned forward, rapt.

"She shared Captain had just recently finished suing a contractor who'd renovated his guesthouse in Astoria. He claimed that the contractor had cut corners, buying cheaper materials than what Captain ordered. He had pictures of the shoddy, rushed work, and even comparisons of the pieces he ordered versus what was installed."

I took a long gulp of my iced tea. "And did he win?"

"He did. Took the contractor for everything he had."

Drumming my fingers on the table, I thought about that. It didn't sound like the generous multimillionaire I'd grown to know throughout this investigation. "He definitely didn't need the money, though," I mused aloud.

"My thoughts exactly," the chief said. "So it wasn't a surprise when Fallon said he wrote a check to the defendant's wife after it was all over. Fallon disclosed that the major nail in the contractor's coffin was when his wife testified against him, told the court that he'd shared his plans to rip off Captain with her."

"So the lawsuit was likely personal." I widened my eyes. "I think we need to talk to this woman."

"I've already got her name," the chief said. "I'm going to speak with her tomorrow evening. She's in Astoria. Want to come with?"

My breath stuck in my throat. "Of course."

A momentary worry caught me as I wondered if Callie would be okay. But she'd been so excited ever since she'd gotten the bed-and-breakfast news off her chest that I figured she'd be fine watching the shop for one more day.

"Oh, and maybe tell Mom that we should move dinner to here on Saturday. I think we should turn it into a moving party for Callie. She's going to manage The Gull's Nest starting next week."

The chief's face brightened. "Ah, she finally told you."

I gasped. "You two already knew?"

He shifted his weight. "She told us about a week ago. She was terrified to let you down."

My anger at being left out of the family secret softened and I said, "She didn't need to worry. I'm ecstatic for her."

The chief reached out and squeezed my hand. "As we told her you would be."

I felt tears prick at the corners of my eyes at the reminder of all the changes coming my way. "Okay, Astoria tomorrow evening. I'll be ready."

But as I glanced inside and caught sight of Asher, I realized that there was something else waiting for us in Astoria: Lyle and the truth about what happened to Asher.

The way I'd dragged him out of the museum, away from Lyle on Monday still haunted me. We'd decided that we would go back once we were ready, but I wasn't sure I'd ever be *ready* to say goodbye to him.

Asher deserved to be at peace, and prolonging it was selfish of me. Just as I couldn't stand in the way of Callie's happiness, I couldn't be the reason Asher wasn't moving on.

This time, I needed to do the right thing in Astoria and talk to Lyle Hulquist.

19

Asher and I went out to the cannery that night while Owen helped Callie pack. Getting to the bottom of what had been bothering Callie reminded me I still had another mystery waiting to be solved, one that might help the chief and me as we closed in on Captain's murderer: Genny's final vision.

I'd given her as much time as I could. I needed her to open up about what she'd seen in that fourth vision. Also, I wanted to see if the local ghosts had any idea what could stop Trip from leaving the sail loft warehouse.

The air was still humid as the sun dipped lower in the sky. The old concrete structure of the abandoned cannery smelled even more dusty and earthy as the concrete cooled after a long day of baking in the direct sunlight. Gulls cried in the distance, and the sound of waves crashing against the jagged rocks of the cliff below echoed into the skeletal structure.

Genny was curled up in a ball in the corner again, but she wasn't rocking. Asher said she'd been out and about, only coming back to the cannery when I said I needed to talk to her. It seemed like much of her initial fear had subsided. I hoped it would be enough.

"Hi, Genny," I said, crossing my legs so I could sit next to her. The concrete was cool on the back of my bare legs, and I wished I'd changed from shorts to long pants.

She looked up at me, her eyes only narrowing for a fraction of a second. We were making progress for sure.

"Hey," she mumbled, looking back down at her transparent hands.

"It's time. I need you to describe the murder scene from your last vision. I've been helping with this case, so I might've met one of the people in the vision. I could either identify the killer or save the victim, or both."

She shook as her fingers grasped at a chain around her neck, and she pulled a gold locket out from her dress collar. She clenched the small metal pendant like it was a lifeline.

Asher settled next to me. He placed a hand on Genny's knee, thanks to a green tourmaline stone I knew he kept on him at all times.

"I had a locket like that," he said, his low voice smooth and safe. "My niece Maggie gave it to me before I left for deployment. She put a picture of her on one side and my nephew Ben on the other."

Genny's fingers smoothed over the metal. It was an improvement over the death grip she'd had on the object only seconds earlier. She flipped open her locket and peeked at the pictures inside.

"Mine has my father and grandfather inside," she said. "My grandfather gave it to me when I turned twenty-one," she whispered, her body language calming. "Where's yours?" she asked.

Asher touched his neck. I knew the one chain around his neck belonged to his army tags because they had been found on his remains when they'd been exhumed.

"I don't know what happened to my locket, to be honest with you. I never took it off, but it's not here with me now, so …" He shrugged.

"Oh," Genny said.

Asher lifted his chin toward Genny, encouraging me to try again.

"I know it's scary and sad," I said carefully, "but if it could help us stop another person from dying, it's worth it, right?"

She nodded. Gulping out of habit.

I pushed back my shoulders in preparation. "Okay. Don't even think about the actual murder just yet. Can you describe either of the people in your vision?"

Genny closed her eyes. She held up a hand and wobbled it from side to side. "I can't see either of their faces, but they're both young men. I can tell that. They both have shortly cropped hair. The killer has lighter brown hair than the victim. They're both wearing white T-shirts."

I frowned. Young men. That didn't make sense, given our current case. The only young man who I'd had any contact with during this case was Matt, Captain's young assistant. He had dark brown hair that was close-cropped. *Was his life in danger?* He had an alibi, so he couldn't have been the murderer.

Chewing on my lip, I realized that the description alone would not be enough. I'd hoped to spare Genny from having to tell us what happened in the scene, but it couldn't be avoided.

"Genny," I said carefully, "can you describe the murder?" Eyes still closed, she winced, so I added, "You don't have to go into too much detail."

Genny's breathing slowed. She pressed the pads of her fingers together like she was trying to ground herself. "It's early morning. The birds are chirping up a storm. It seems like spring. They're in the forest. There's a ton of fresh growth. At first, I can only see the victim. He's walking, admiring things like he's saying goodbye. He stops to run his hand along a large trunk of a fallen tree. It looks like lightning struck it. But in that moment …" She stopped and seemed to gather all her strength. "In that moment, someone comes up behind him and hits him over the head with a large rock." A tear slid down her cheek. She peeked open her eyes, one at a time.

My mouth opened in shock. A forest. A tree trunk struck by lightning. A blow to the back of the head. It all sounded like the details of Asher's death.

I blinked so my thoughts might line up correctly. And then my gaze tiptoed over to Asher. His expression was almost unreadable. I couldn't tell if that was because he was too in shock to feel anything or if he was feeling everything all at once and couldn't settle on just one emotion.

"That sounds like …" Asher whispered but petered out before he could say what we were both thinking.

The rest of the ghosts were clueless, showing me he'd only shared the story of that dead tree trunk near where he was buried, with me.

"What if the vision isn't something that is going to

happen, but something that already has?" I spoke the question more to myself than anything, but Genny answered.

"That's never happened before. I always saw things before they happened." She crossed her arms in front of her, then immediately let them drop into her lap. "Then again, I never had a repeating vision before this one, so I guess anything's possible."

Swallowing to buy myself another second before having to say this out loud, I pressed my fingers onto the concrete to ground myself. "Genny, I think what you saw was Asher's murder." Even with all the preparation, my voice still cracked over the sentence.

Asher stared at Genny as a look of horror crossed her face.

"Genny, was the man who got hit over the head wearing a locket like yours? Army tags? Can you see anything like that?" he asked, a desperate tightness to his questions.

She closed her eyes for a moment, and then, after an excruciating second, she said, "Yes. He's wearing a couple chains around his neck. A gold one and one that looks like that." She pointed to the chain Asher's army tags hung from around his ghostly neck.

Suddenly an icy fear clenched at my chest, and I surveyed Asher to make sure he wasn't fading away. But we'd known all of this already. We knew he'd been up in the woods; we knew it was likely the night before or morning of when he was supposed to deploy, and we knew someone had hit him on the back of the head. We also knew that Lyle had brown hair, slightly lighter than Asher's dark brown hair. It all clicked. We just needed to hear from Lyle why he did it.

Relaxing a bit, I thought back through the other visions.

The wet footprints on a boardwalk, the rosemary sprig, the letter, and Asher's death.

"Genny, maybe you're not supposed to help us solve Captain's murder, but Asher's," I said hopefully. "Have you thought about that letter, the third vision? Do you know where that might be?" I had no idea what would be inside the letter, but it was obviously imperative for us to find if we hoped to understand why Lyle had killed Asher.

"Yes." Genny nodded, then shook her head. "I mean, I thought about it, and I have no idea. I haven't seen a letter like that, with wax used as a seal, in … ages."

That was when I realized I *had*.

The box Riley had, full of letters from Catherine to Hannah, had all been closed using wax. Most of the wax had been peeled off to be reused, but the signs were there. A few letters had drips of wax or residue left over, even after all these years. One or two of the letters had the wax still attached. And all of it was green.

When Genny had first told us about her vision, I'd thought it was about Captain Westover's case, so I hadn't even thought to connect it with the letters Riley and I had been reading through. But with the revelation of her final vision, that it was likely Asher's death that she'd been seeing for years, it made sense that the letter would be somewhere in the box Riley and I had been searching through.

"I think it's in the box of letters Riley has," I told Asher.

He steepled his fingers in thought. "We had self-gumming letters at the point Catherine would've been writing to my si—" He cut himself off. "But it's very much like Catherine to stick to the flashy wax seal. She was all about appearances." He waved a hand at me. "Never mind. That checks out."

"Good," I said. "I'll find the letter tomorrow, then." I looked at Genny. "You said it has a green wax seal and a bent right corner?"

She confirmed it did.

A shiver rushed over me as the breeze flowed through the abandoned cannery building. "I'd better get home," I said, rubbing my hands up and down my arms. I stood, saying a quick goodbye to the spirits. Asher stuck close by my side. Once we were out in the parking lot, I said, "Are you okay?"

"It's nothing we didn't already know." A hard swallow followed.

I agreed. "But it's still a lot, hearing it described like that." I reached forward, knowing he would push energy through his hand so we could touch. He did, his fingers linking with mine for a second, squeezing tight.

An electricity flowed through us that made me want to pull him close, but I knew I couldn't. Because I could see the same need for answers, for closure flowing through him as it did when my mom was researching. He needed to know, which meant that it was only a matter of time before I had to say goodbye.

"I'll just be happy when we have the truth," he whispered, knowing what that would mean for both of us.

"I'm sure we will tomorrow." I couldn't bear to look at him, so I studied the sunset instead.

It was possible that this would be the last sunset we would ever watch together.

20

The next morning, I texted Riley bright and early.

Any chance you have some free time today to look through the letters? I'd be happy to come to you this time.

I'd never been to Riley's house. We had always either met at the tea shop or a coffee shop in Sun City. The prospect of seeing Riley's home made me nervous for some reason, as though it might give me too clear a window into his life. Would I like what I saw, or would it make me see him differently than I already did?

Riley was an early riser, so he answered almost immediately.

I don't have a class until 1:00 today, so I'll just be grading essays until then. You're more than welcome to come over.

I scrambled out of bed and got ready as quickly as I could, explaining to Callie where I was going.

"Are you sure about this?" Callie asked as I gathered my

purse and keys. She placed a skeptical hand on her hip and narrowed her eyes at me.

I nodded, even though I wasn't. "I have to know what's inside that letter. It could free Genny to move on if we figure out what the connection between her and Asher's death is." I scratched at my nose. "Plus, I'm going to swing by Destiny's place and see if she can help with our Trip conundrum. I texted her the other day and she said she would ask around to see if any of the other mediums she knows have ideas about how to free him."

Callie studied me for too long. "Are you at least bringing Asher with you?" she asked, searching around like she'd only just noticed he wasn't anywhere to be found.

"He doesn't want to be involved in the letter business, just in case," I explained. "But I told him I'd call him to me once I had a moment alone in Astoria."

Callie sighed. "Okay. At least take a scone for the road." She wrapped up a freshly baked scone.

"Thanks," I said, clutching the warm treat. Then it was my chance to study her. "Are *you* sure you're okay with me leaving for the day?" By the time I got back from Sun City, I would leave with the chief for Astoria, which meant Callie was here all by herself for the day.

She snorted. "Of course I am. I love hanging here, especially now that I know this is my last week before I move to The Gull's Nest. I'm soaking it in."

Taking my scone and a mug of my new Sunset blend tea, I drove south.

My tea and scone were long gone by the time I stopped at Destiny's shop, The Herbal Witch. It wasn't until I approached the front door that I remembered Destiny rarely opened this early. A few months earlier, when I'd first found her shop, her hours had been much later. But a quick check of the sign in the window told me she was open, and when I pulled on the handle, the door opened easily.

The small space was full of crystals, tinctures, and plants. The drying flowers and plants hanging from the ceiling made me automatically feel at home, like I was in my backyard shed drying leaves and flowers for my tea blends. I closed my eyes as I pulled in a deep breath that smelled of the earthy, floral scent that sat heavily in the space.

"I thought you might come in today," Destiny said, causing me to open my eyes as she walked out of the back room. She held a potted plant in one hand. The soil was dark and moist, like she'd just watered it.

I fiddled with my purse strap. "I'm glad you're open."

She winked at me, telling me it was a distinct possibility that she'd opened just because she knew I was coming.

"I don't suppose you found out anything more about the kind of spirits who might be trapped inside objects, like the one in the building I called you about?" I asked, adding, "Or how to free the other spirit trapped inside with it?"

Destiny set down the plant and motioned to a sitting area full of large pillows and freshly cut flowers. "I did a little asking around after you texted. The consensus between the mediums I spoke with is that you'll need to get the spirit to leave the building before the one who's stuck can go anywhere."

That made sense.

"It's not going to be so easy, though," Destiny added. "Spirits who inhabit a building or object in the afterlife are often those who have such a small amount of a soul left that they don't even appear as a ghost most of the time. They're the kind who've either had something terrible happen to them, or they did the terrible things." She swallowed.

My heart raced at the thought of confronting such a spirit. "But how do I talk to a spirit who's haunting a building? Do I just go yell at the walls?"

I wanted to chuckle at the image, but very little about this was funny. The eerie feeling I got whenever I thought of that sail loft made me sure the spirit trapped inside was no laughing matter.

"There is a spirit in there," Destiny said. "And they'll be able to show up as a ghost for a short period of time. It's just not their regular form. Worse comes to worst, you can just yell at the walls, but I have a feeling that if you talk to the spirit, they'll show their face."

I thanked her and said goodbye, plugging Riley's address into my phone and heading in that direction. His house was only a short drive from Destiny's shop. The place was impressive. It was a modern design, all clean lines and simple colors. I pressed the digital doorbell and cocked an eyebrow as it lit up.

"Hey, Rosie. I'm coming." Riley's voice spilled out from the device, making me jump. I peered into it, wondering if there was a camera in there as well. A moment later, he opened the door, a smile on his face.

He wore a button-up shirt and shorts, relaxed but professional enough to teach later. The smell of coffee wafted out through the front door.

"Come in." He stepped aside, ushering me in.

The space differed from what I expected. Well, it was

different from my house, for sure. Where my old Victorian was all cozy rooms, dark wood, and various art, Riley's space was open and stark. I couldn't tell if he'd just moved in or if he simply preferred minimalism. There was a single couch, a large television on the opposite wall, and his marble kitchen counter held one bowl full of fruits and veggies. It was a far cry from my kitchen, cluttered with tchotchkes and baking paraphernalia.

"Your place is really nice. How long have you lived here?" I asked, scanning the space.

"About five years," he said.

Oh, so he hadn't just moved in. Which meant that he was super into minimalism. My place probably made him feel crowded in the same way his left me feeling disconnected.

"I have to admit. I was surprised to get your text this morning," he said as he led me toward the kitchen table where he had a laptop open, the box of letters next to it. "You kind of freaked out last time." His brown eyes held mine.

I cringed. "I know. I'm sorry. There's just … more to all of this than I can explain at the moment."

Sadness welled inside of me at the realization that I couldn't tell him any of it. Riley had become a good friend over the past few months. He was a nice guy. Would he understand or think I was crazy?

His mouth tipped up into an accepting smile. "I'm here for you. Anytime you need to talk."

He grabbed hold of my hand, squeezing it tight. My eyes flashed up to meet his. When we'd first met months ago, he'd told me he was just getting out of a relationship and wasn't ready to commit to anything new. I wondered if that was changing.

Riley cleared his throat. "Look, Rosie, there's something I need to—" A notification on his computer interrupted him, and he scowled at the screen for a moment while I internally freaked out.

He needed to tell me something? I guessed from the fragmented sentence. Piecing that together with the way he'd just taken my hand, the room felt as if it were shifting around me. Was he going to say he was finally ready for a relationship? I didn't want to hurt his feelings, but I wasn't in any condition to decide about my love life at the moment.

Desperate for a way out of whatever conversation he wanted to have, I whispered, "Do you mind if I look through these?" I gestured toward the box.

He glanced up from his screen and blinked. "Oh, sorry. Just dealing with a student question. Yes, be my guest. I might just take care of this really quickly." He flicked his fingers toward the laptop screen.

"Sure. No problem." I exhaled in relief, at least getting a small reprieve from whatever talk he wanted to have.

The *click clack* of Riley's fingers on his keyboard started up as I leafed through the letters in the box. As I searched, I kept my eyes peeled for the one with the green wax and the bent corner. It only took me a few minutes before I pulled it out, staring at it like it might not be real.

"Did you find something?" Riley asked, his attention caught on me and the letter I clutched.

"Um. I don't know yet." I blinked as I thought up a lie. "I just thought this one was interesting because it has all the wax left on the seal, unlike the others."

Riley nodded, looking back at his laptop screen.

With shaking fingers, I opened the letter. This was it. The one from Genny's vision.

It was yet another letter from Catherine.

Dear Hannah,

I must say that your last letter broke my heart. I am so sorry you went through that harrowing experience. I had no idea. I, myself, have never been cornered by a man like that, though I have heard many a story of other women I know dealing with the same unwanted advances. Even worse that it was someone so close to your family!

I am glad you finally told me, though I admit I wish you had opened up back when it happened, while you still lived in Pebble Cove, because then I could have wrapped you up in a tight hug. But I understand how uncomfortable it must have been, and that you needed time and space away from the difficult experience to finally talk about it (or write about it, at least).

As for your worries that telling Asher the night before he was set to deploy was part of the reason he deserted, I do not think you can put that on yourself. His actions are entirely his own. And as much as I know your family has struggled with his decision, I have to believe that the Asher I have grown to know over the years would have wanted to know if his big sister had been put in such an upset-ting situation, by someone so close. But it must've been hard for him to hear, and I can understand why he might not have confronted him.

That being said, you are spot on about the man's character and should advise your father not to put him in charge of the Benson Fishing Company. A man like that is only good for ruining lives. Nothing positive will come of his involvement in your family's company.

Best wishes,
Your friend,
Catherine

The tone of the letter thoroughly surprised me. Catherine, until that point, was catty and gossipy. But in this letter, she was subdued and supportive. Whatever Hannah shared in her last letter must've been hard for her to write. It sounded like she'd been cornered by a man. And the person who'd done the cornering was someone close to her family and whom her father was considering handing over the running of the company.

Lyle Hulquist.

The unwanted advances, and Hannah's confession that she told Asher the night before he left, answered the last few lingering questions. Hannah worried that telling Asher had played a part in his disappearance. And even though her reasoning was off, she wasn't necessarily wrong. A gut feeling told me that Asher had gone to confront Lyle the morning he was supposed to leave.

Had Asher threatened to tell his father, Lyle's boss? Did Lyle kill Ash to keep his secret safe? The motivation to kill Asher before he left for war, when he very well could've perished in battle, now made total sense.

The reality of the situation settled over me like a concrete block. I finally knew all of the details of Asher's murder. I inhaled, holding the breath in my lungs until it burned. I let it go slowly, gaining a little control over my emotions.

"Rosie, are you okay?" Riley's voice broke through my thoughts.

I glanced over at him. His eyebrows pulled together.

"What's in that letter?" He motioned to the paper I still held with shaking fingers.

I cleared my throat to reset myself. "Oh, it's kind of awful, actually. A close family friend, someone who worked for her father, cornered Hannah with some unwanted attention."

"Lyle?" Riley asked, sitting up straight.

I fidgeted with the bent corner of the letter. "It sounds like it."

"Whoa." Riley sat back in his chair.

"Yeah." I mirrored his body position. "And she told Asher about it before he left for deployment. Which I think means that when Asher went to confront Lyle about his inappropriate behavior around Hannah, Lyle killed him."

Riley and I sat in silence for a beat.

"So that's it. You solved it." Riley puffed out his cheeks.

"We solved it," I amended. "I couldn't have done this without you."

He nodded absentmindedly. "It's weird. I don't know what I expected, but this seems so anticlimactic."

I snorted out a laugh. "Tell me about it."

In a way, he was right. Finding the killer after all this time felt like it deserved balloons and streamers. On the other hand—and this was the part I couldn't tell him—there was nothing anticlimactic about this news at all. Because this piece of information would change everything. Once I shared it with Asher, it would alter my life forever.

Checking my watch, I said, "Oh gosh. I'd better get going." I had to meet Chief Clemenson in just over an hour for our trip up to Astoria.

Riley smiled tightly and stood. "Well, this is … weird." He ran his hand through his hair.

I hugged my arms around myself and nodded. I didn't know what to say.

"Do you mind if I still come by this Friday?" he asked. "Even though we don't have any mysteries to solve anymore?"

Smiling, I said, "Of course." The truth was, I was staring down so many goodbyes right now that not having to say goodbye to Riley, too, felt like a minor consolation. "I'm looking forward to it." Glancing back at the box, I said, "Do you mind if I borrow that letter for a bit? I'll give it back when I see you on Friday. I just want to share it with … my mom."

Riley plucked the letter from where I'd set it. "No problem."

"Thanks." I clutched it tightly once he handed it over.

Riley opened his mouth, and worry filled me that he might bring up the untouched subject from earlier. Maybe my concern was written on my face because he clamped his lips together and said, "I'll walk you out."

21

D riving up to Astoria with the chief took a lot less time than my boat trip with Keller and his crew. And while I didn't foresee getting seasick, it was decidedly less scenic and held none of the adventure I'd felt crossing the bar.

"I heard from the IP lawyer this morning," the chief said conversationally as he drove.

I arched an eyebrow. "Yeah, what did he have to say?"

"Captain Westover was trying to file patents for his sail design." The way Clemenson said this, flat and worried, made me realize that this didn't bode well for the Rickster.

"He hadn't done that yet?" I asked.

"He didn't think it was important when he and the Rickster started the company," the chief said. "But apparently, recently, Captain became worried that someone might try to use the design and he was looking at filing a patent. The lawyer informed Captain that since the original designs had been publicly disclosed, and he was well past any grace period for filing, he would have to make significant modifications to the product to improve upon the original design. Then he might be able to argue that it was eligible for a patent. But what bothers me is thinking about another person with access to those original designs." He shot me a knowing glance.

"The Rickster," I said with a sigh.

"Along with the postcard we found, it's not looking good for him." The chief stretched his neck from side to side.

"What postcard?" I asked, remembering the one in Rickster's houseboat from Cap.

The chief winced. "A few months ago, Rick sent Captain a postcard with the words, *Pay up or die* written on it. He told us that the monthly payments hadn't been coming for about four months, and he'd just gotten a postcard from Cap in Hawaii, so the guy obviously had the money to pay him."

That must've been the postcard I'd seen in the Rickster's houseboat. "So he sent one back that said *Pay up or die*?" I puffed out my cheeks.

"He said it was a joke." The chief lifted his hands off the steering wheel for a moment to show he didn't understand either. "He was adamant that it was just how they talked to each other. Do or die. Say yes or die. Something about when they were younger." The chief shrugged. "But if Rick helped design the sail, he probably felt entitled to the money, especially if his monthly payments hadn't been coming. Maybe he threatened to sell the design."

I agreed. It was yet one more strike against the Rickster.

The chief and I arrived at Rachel Southard's house a short while later. She lived in a small one-story in a neighborhood that had seen better days, much like her house.

The paint could use a fresh coat, the porch steps sagged when we stepped onto them, and one of her gutters along the front of the house was hanging at an angle.

In contrast to her house, Rachel was bright-eyed and put together when she answered the door. She appeared to be in her thirties. Her wide smile felt genuine, like she was happy in a deep-down, complete kind of way. She was pretty, with curly brown hair and dark eyes.

"Hello, you must be Chief Clemenson." She held out her hand, and Raymond shook it.

"Thank you for meeting with me," he said. "This is my daughter, Rosemary." He gestured toward me.

I grinned at our host. "Hi, thank you for letting me tag along."

She waved a hand. "No problem. Anything for Captain. He's done so much to help me."

She led us inside, asking if we wanted anything to drink. We declined, sitting around her kitchen table, poised to listen. The interior was much like Rachel, put together and radiant. It was cozy and compact but cleaned to a shine. It was obvious she took great pride in her space.

"You said Captain did so much to help you. What exactly has he done?" The chief pulled out his notepad and poised his pen over the page, ready to take notes.

Rachel widened her eyes. "What hasn't he done? He helped me get away from that creep I was married to, once and for all."

I inhaled sharply, but if the chief was surprised, he didn't let on.

"How so?" he asked.

She puffed out her cheeks. "Where to start? Well, I used

to help Gabe with his renovation business. I would schedule his time, order materials for him, and sometimes even help with things like painting and sealing. Stuff I felt comfortable with. One day, when we were almost done with Cap's guest-house, I was there painting. Gabe had gone off to get materials for the next job he had lined up. I was doing the final coat of paint and I was crying." At this, Rachel gripped her left wrist with her right hand and squeezed down tight as if she were uncomfortable and needed to ground herself. "Gabe hit me a lot. And when he wasn't hitting me, he would yell at me and make me feel stupid. He'd pushed me into a wall that morning, and my shoulder ached. Not to mention my soul, that ached too. Captain came inside to see the progress and heard me crying. He asked what was wrong and listened to everything."

The chief jotted down notes.

Rachel continued. "He was so lovely, such a good listener. I told him about how I felt stuck. I wanted to divorce Gabe but felt sure he would take me to the cleaners and leave me with nothing since it was his company. I wasn't sure how to prove I was an integral part of the business. Without hesitation, Cap offered to set me up with his lawyer so I could get some legal advice about leaving Gabe. When I told him I couldn't afford that, he told me he would pay for it." She sniffed as she got emotional all over again. "It was the first kindness I'd received in far too long. After that, I spilled to him all the shortcuts Gabe took in his work and how he'd ordered less-expensive materials so he could pocket the difference. Cap thanked me profusely and started his own lawsuit against Gabe at the same time I filed for divorce. He even helped me find this place." She regarded the house proudly. "I know it's not much, but it's the first thing I've owned without Gabe."

Her love for her sanctuary showed. Suddenly, the difference between the interior and exterior of her house made sense. She might not know how to fix a gutter or build a new porch, but she took great care of what she could control.

Chief Clemenson inhaled. "That had to be a lot of stress and anger for Gabe. You said he was violent toward you. Do you think he might've taken out his anger on Captain?"

Rachel jutted her chin back. "Like he might've been the one to kill him? I mean … maybe."

"Do you know where Gabe was last Thursday night, around ten o'clock?" The chief cut the air with his palm immediately after asking the question. "Sorry, of course you probably don't. You're not married anymore."

Rachel shook her head but then stopped. "Actually, I do." She blinked, like this revelation surprised her just as much as it would us. "I saw him at a bar downtown. I was there meeting a friend and we got to talking, stayed later than I planned to. But when she and I were leaving, I saw Gabe was at the bar, nursing a whiskey. He didn't see me, and I got out of there fast once I spotted him."

"What time was that?" Clemenson asked, writing it down in his notebook.

"Nine thirty?" Rachel wrinkled her nose. "Maybe a little later."

The chief nodded. "Thank you. I'll check into that, but it sounds like it couldn't have been him if he was all the way up here at that time of night."

Rachel cringed. "I'm sorry."

"That's okay," the chief said softly. He closed his notepad. "One more thing. Do you know of anyone in Cap's life who was a scuba diver?"

Rachel thought hard about this. "Just his old assistant, Matt."

"Old assistant?" I blurted.

The chief leaned forward in surprise.

"Yeah, he fired Matt about two weeks ago," Rachel said.

The chief and I blinked at each other.

Sensing she might be wrong, Rachel added, "At least, that had been Captain's plan. He complained Matt was always asking for more. He kept overstepping his bounds too. Like, he unilaterally decided to stop sending payments to Captain's business partner, without even asking him. But if Matt's still working there, maybe Captain changed his mind."

So Matt was the one who'd been to blame for the Rickster's payments stopping. The chief scribbled something down in his notebook, probably citing that same point.

"I don't think he did," the chief said, his eyes narrowing.

"What if Matt stole his sail designs and then took care of Cap when he confronted him about it?" I said, knowing the chief was probably thinking along the same lines but wouldn't say it without proof.

Rachel scoffed. "I wouldn't put it past him. That guy was a piece of work. All about moving up. He always talked like he would take over the company someday. Entitled little jerk. Cap worried he might've stolen the designs, but he said his business partner could help him with the design changes they needed to file patents, and give Matt a proper run for his money if he did try to start his own business using the designs. He was talking to an IP lawyer about it all. I wasn't worried, but it looks like I should've been." She flinched. "Annoying as Matt is, I didn't think for a second he would resort to murder."

"I hope you don't blame yourself. You couldn't have known." Clemenson stood. "Thank you for your help, Rachel. I'll let you know if we have any more questions." He set his hat back on his head as we exited her house.

We climbed into his SUV.

"Cap came to the Rickster for help," I whispered.

Raymond nodded sadly. "And Matt must've known he would. He was in Pebble Cove, waiting."

"But he had an alibi," I said.

The chief exhaled. "His mother. I should've known better than to take her word. Parents will usually do anything to protect their children."

We sat in silence for a beat.

"Rosemary, I need to go talk to the Astoria police chief and coordinate with him about getting out an APB for Matt Barker. I'm not sure they'll be so keen to have a civilian around. Do you mind waiting in the car?" He grimaced in apology as he started driving.

The huge bridge loomed ahead of us. My thoughts strayed to Lyle Hulquist. Now that I knew the truth, I didn't technically need to see him anymore, but in the hours since I'd read Catherine's letter, an anger had built inside me, one I wanted to get off my chest.

"Actually, I heard good things about the maritime museum," I said. "Could you drop me off? I can hang out there until you're done."

The chief exhaled in relief. He dropped me off, and I waved goodbye, hoping they found Matt.

I walked toward the entrance but didn't go inside. I didn't want to chance the museum staff recognizing me from Monday and making me leave just in case I yelled about pineapples again.

So once the chief's SUV was out of sight, I veered to the side of the building and sat on the nearest bench facing the river. Turning my moonstone ring so I could touch the stone with my thumb, I called Lyle Hulquist's name three times.

He appeared next to me, ghostly arms splayed out wide, and eyes searching frantically for whatever had moved him. When his gaze landed on me, his surprised expression darkened.

In that moment, I wished I'd thought to bring some salt with me. With the quick turnaround between Riley's house and the chief picking me up, I'd forgotten to grab any.

Lyle must've been an old man when he died because his hair was white and his posture stooped. That must've been why it had taken Asher a moment to recognize him the other day. But I could easily picture his hair being a brown shade lighter than Asher's.

Gathering all the inner strength that I possessed, I leveled him with just as angry a scowl as he was directing at me. With a quick check to make sure no one else was around, I said, "I need answers, and you're going to give them to me. Sit."

The self-assured, strong person who gave those orders was the Rosie I'd always dreamed I could be, I realized with a start. In those daydreams, I never thought I would use my newfound confidence to boss around ghosts, but I enjoyed the fact that I could stand up for myself and those I loved.

If Lyle was surprised I could see him, he didn't show it. He'd already seen me talking to Asher on Monday in the museum, so he'd had plenty of time to get over any shock he might've felt. He sat next to me, though I noticed he stayed on the farthest edge of the bench, like he was worried I could reach out and grab him.

Pulling out the letter I'd borrowed from Riley's box, I wafted it between us.

"I want the truth about what you did to Asher Benson." My tone was level, no nonsense.

Lyle Hulquist's ghostly shoulders sagged forward. He let his head fall forward into his palms.

"I had a feeling this was why I was still here," he said, his voice gravelly, as if his throat was covered in the same barnacles that clung to the hulls of boats.

"You think?" I scoffed, incredulous.

He held up his transparent hands. "I've made a lot of mistakes in my life. I'll own up to that."

"Mistakes?" I spat out the question. "You call murder a mistake?"

At this, Lyle's eyes flew open. "Murder? I didn't kill Asher."

I snorted. "Sure. You just took over his job managing the business once he was gone, hated that he was your boss when he didn't know as much as you, and came on to his married sister." I waved the letter at him. "What ... did he come after you once he found out? Was that the last straw and then you snapped, deciding not to wait to see if he died in the war?"

Lyle blinked. "Look, young lady. I didn't kill Asher, and I most definitely didn't make any unwanted advances toward Hannah. She was a married woman."

"I have the proof. It all points to you." I set my shoulders in defiance to show I wouldn't back down.

"I didn't," he snarled, then sat back, calming down. "But I know who did, and it's a secret I took to the grave."

22

It took me a moment to get my bearings.

Lyle wasn't Asher's killer? Suddenly the Columbia River rushing by wasn't the only thing moving. The whole world felt like it was tipping around me.

"What?" I croaked out.

Lyle's jaw clenched tight.

But before he could even speak, I knew. The letter clutched in my hand held the clue, one I didn't see until that moment. *A close family friend,* Catherine had said when talking about the man who'd cornered Hannah. Then, when talking about Asher, she'd written, *It must've been hard for him to hear, and I can understand why he might not have confronted him.*

"Charlie." The name was a whisper on my lips.

Lyle nodded.

Every fact I'd overlooked until that moment—because I'd seen Charlie as Asher had, as his best friend—came crashing down on me. Charlie was the son Asher's father had always wanted. He was great with boats. He didn't have a family of his own, so he came home with Asher on breaks and holidays. Charlie often said he wished he had Asher's life.

What if he got Asher out of the way so he could?

What if he was planning on waiting until after they got back from the war, but Asher confronted him about his inappropriate behavior toward Hannah? What if Charlie took his opportunity while he could, letting everyone think Asher had deserted?

"How'd you find out?" I asked Lyle.

He flinched. "It's not a flattering story. I guess it's better than you thinking I'm a murderer, though." He leaned back. "When I was younger, I didn't have much. Got by some days by doing a little light pick pocketing. It was a hard habit to break. So even after I was in charge, once Asher was gone, I would still find the urge to 'inspect' the lockers. Things went missing all the time in an industry like ours. I never took anything from men who I respected. Anyway, when Charlie got back from the war, Archie hired him for one of the crews, said he would have to work his way up and gain the respect of the fishermen. I saw right through him, though. He was gunning for my job."

I angled my body toward him as I listened.

"So one day, I was poking around in his jacket. He had a locket, one I'd seen Asher showing off because his niece had given it to him. He cherished that thing. Inside were the same pictures of Asher's niece and nephew he'd shown us when he'd first received the gift. I didn't know why Charlie would have it." Lyle sighed. "Charlie caught me snooping. I confronted him about the locket. He spat out some lie about how Asher had given it to him before they left, just in case he didn't make it, but it didn't make sense since, at that point, we all thought Asher had deserted." Lyle's face clouded over. "I only had to push a little before he spilled everything. It was almost like he wanted to tell someone."

A shiver ran down my back.

Lyle continued. "Charlie explained about Asher coming after him, furious about what Hannah had told him. He described his plan to get Asher out of the way by making his family believe he'd deserted, all of it." Lyle made a throat-clearing noise. "But then he proposed a new plan, one where the two of us took over the business, got rich instead of working to make Archie even richer."

I swallowed. "What was that plan?"

"My job was just to sabotage small things here and there. Break an engine, miss a job, etcetera. If the company wasn't doing well, Charlie could go to Archie and tell him he could save it." Any pride left in Lyle melted away. He looked down in embarrassment. "Archie would let him take over. He would get it back up to where it was performing before, if not better, and then we'd cut Archie out for good, keeping everything for ourselves."

I bit at my cheek. "But that didn't work, did it?"

Lyle swallowed. "It did until it didn't. My sabotage worked. The company was in trouble. Charlie stepped up and offered to save it if Archie would sell. Archie did. But Charlie didn't foresee the Great Depression. Once that hit, he couldn't recover the already failing company. He was going to cut his losses and sell off the fleet, but Archie was a sentimental fool. He bought the company back from Charlie, thought he could save it." Lyle shook his head. "He sank all of his money into it. They ended up destitute." Pain contorted Lyle's features. "As mad as I was at Archie in those days, mostly for putting Asher in charge of me when the boy always had his nose in a book, I felt bad for them. Archie wasn't a bad man, maybe a little greedy, but not bad. Charlie, however, he was evil."

"What happened to him after that?" I asked.

Lyle shrugged. "Lived his life, I guess. Never really saw much more of the man. I started on a new fishing crew. Left that behind me. Well, as much as I could. Charlie insisted I keep the locket. At first I was happy to have something valuable. But I later realized he probably gave it to me so he could pin the murder on me if anyone ever got close to figuring out what he'd done." Lyle wrinkled his nose. "I gave it to my granddaughter on her twenty-first birthday."

My eyes went wide. Genny's story about her locket, how her grandfather had given it to her on the same birthday was too much of a coincidence. "Your granddaughter wouldn't happen to be named Genevieve, would she?"

He cocked his head. "Yes, though she always went by Genny."

That clicked into place like a locket snapping shut. The locket Genny wore had been Asher's. That was why she kept seeing his death. He'd died wearing it.

I pointed an accusatory finger at him. "Lyle, Genny's spirit hasn't been able to move on because of that locket."

"Genny's still here?" He breathed out the question. "Oh, my dear Genny." His eyes squeezed shut once more.

"Ever since you gave it to her, she's been having visions of what really happened to Asher Benson," I explained.

"Her visions." He tapped at his temple. "I forgot about those."

"Well, she hasn't been able to. She's had to watch Charlie kill Asher repeatedly." I crossed my arms.

Lyle stood, his face and body contorted in a deep pain. "I have to go talk to her. To tell her I'm sorry."

"She's in Pebble Cove," I said, unconvinced that would help, but not about to stop him.

"Thank you," he said, his fingers clenching together in fists like he truly meant it.

Before he left, I saw an opportunity. This mystery might be solved, but there was still poor Trip, unable to leave. I wondered if Lyle could help.

"Lyle, you know a lot about Astoria, right?" I motioned to the museum behind us, where he seemed to spend a lot of his time.

He nodded.

"What do you know about the sail loft building?" I asked, pointing toward Captain's warehouse.

Lyle's eyebrows arched with interest. "Quite a lot, actually."

I sat forward, ready to listen.

"That was our building for close to a decade." He stared up the river like he was imagining a time gone by.

"Our building?" I asked. "You mean, the Benson Fishing Company?"

Lyle bobbed his head. "Yep, same building."

Suddenly I had a pretty good guess about whose spirit haunted that building. A plan formed in my mind. I knew how to set Trip free.

———

THE SUN WAS SETTING, and a chill wafted up off the river. I rubbed my hands up and down my arms as I walked closer to the sail loft, toward the old Benson Fishing Company building.

What had Destiny said about spirits who inhabited buildings or objects instead of showing up as ghosts? *"They are often spirits who have such a small amount of a soul left that they don't even appear as a ghost most of the time. They're the kind who've either had something terrible happen to them or they did the terrible things."*

The latter option sounded like it fit Charlie to a tee. He'd killed his best friend and then ruined the family he'd tried so hard to be a part of. Which meant I was about to summon a very dangerous spirit.

The interior of the sail loft was dark as I approached. Everyone must've gone home already for the evening. I squared my shoulders and stood tall in front of the building.

The streets were empty of people, no one out this late in the industrial part of the docks. And while I knew it was likely because all the businesses on this part of the river walk were closed for the evening, it felt eerie.

A story built up in my head: I was standing in the middle of a deserted town in the Old West, about to stand off with a sharpshooter at high noon, and everyone who had any sense was hidden away.

I was alone.

I clutched the saltshaker I'd bought off a confused server in a restaurant on my way here. If I was going to take on a murdering ghost, I needed some protection.

"Charlie McBride," I called toward the building. The river wind whipped through my short hair. "I know you're in there. Come out and talk to me." I pressed my finger into the moonstone ring until it hurt. I called his name three times. No one appeared.

In the window, I saw Trip's spirit peer outside. He waved to me, smiling in thanks, but from the grimace he wore after that, it didn't seem like he had faith I would succeed.

"Not going to come out, Charlie?" I asked in a mock pout. "Too scared to face me? Too scared to own up to what you did? I guess that makes sense based on what I've learned about you. It sounds just like all you do is hide."

I waited, breath coming in quick gasps as my heart rate rose with each passing second.

The building shuddered. Trip widened his eyes, glancing above him like he wondered if the roof might fall on top of him, not that it could hurt him anymore.

"Oh, come on, Charlie," I said in a calmer voice than I thought I could muster. "That's not going to scare me. Come talk to me. If you're not scared of me or of what you did." I folded my arms in front of myself, wishing I had the physical version of Asher's locket. I needed something to lure him out of the building.

"Rosemary?"

Shivers ran down my arms at the familiar voice. I spun around to see Asher standing behind me.

"Ash, what ... how are you here?" I asked.

He walked forward. "I was worried about you. You never called me like you said you would. I guess once you summon me someplace, I can travel here anytime I want." His boyish grin was full of excitement, until he looked at my expression, my posture, at the salt in my hand. "What are you doing here?"

I hid the salt behind my back. "I'm …" I pointed to the building behind me. "I was trying to help Trip. I was going to get the ghost out of the building. But we don't have to do that. Let's go." My heartbeat skyrocketed. I rushed toward him, wishing he would use his energy to become solid so I could physically push him away.

"Leaving so soon?" a cool voice asked behind me. I dropped the salt I held.

I turned to see a man in his thirties, maybe forties. He appeared to be from the same time period as Trip. But it wasn't Trip. Not by a long shot. This man had cool blue eyes that pierced through me. He had brown hair, just a shade or two lighter than Asher's. His hands rested easily in the pockets of his trousers as he took one step, then another, toward us.

"Charlie? Is that you?" Asher broke into an even bigger smile. He went to move forward but stopped as he looked at me. He cocked his head to the side. "Rosemary, what's wrong?"

Behind him, out of the corner of my eye, I could see Trip step out of the building, tentatively, like a prisoner being set free after serving decades behind bars. But I couldn't celebrate, because everything was about to come tumbling down.

"Ash, you need to leave. Now." A single tear cut a path down my cheek as my watery eyes pleaded with him.

"He doesn't know yet, does he?" Charlie's voice was snakelike, chilling.

Asher's forehead furrowed. "Know what?"

23

Another tear ran down my cheek. "Ash, I can't." The sentence was waterlogged. I sobbed out the words. But it didn't matter.

It was too late. It was all over.

Asher's steel-blue eyes flashed from me to Charlie. "It was you?" He yelled the question first, then said it a second time, quieter, like the truth was sinking in, pulling him under with it. "It was you."

"Oh, don't act so surprised. I always resented you. You knew that." Charlie stepped forward. "I told you I wished I had your life."

"I thought you were joking," Asher said, shaking his head.

"You had everything I wanted. And then you had the gall to punch me in the nose for coming on to your sister. You threatened to tell your father. I couldn't have that. So I followed you the morning we were supposed to leave for deployment."

"You were my best friend," Asher said, the crease between his eyebrows deepening.

Charlie snorted. "Then you obviously know nothing about friendship."

Asher started, like that statement was the finger snap of a hypnotist waking a subject out of a deep sleep. He pressed his shoulders back and met Charlie's glare with one that held so much fury, I wondered if he might try to strangle him. The green tourmaline stone would let him get his hands around his throat at least, but Asher couldn't hurt Charlie, not anymore.

"You're wrong," I called out, swiping under each of my eyes to get rid of the tears still clinging there.

Charlie and Asher turned to face me. Charlie's ghostly jaw clenched tight. But Asher's eyes met mine. He smiled and the laugh lines I loved so much returned one last time.

"You're wrong," I said, Asher's smile contagious. My lips pulled up into a goofy grin. "He knows everything about friendship. He's the best friend I've ever had or will ever have. He's kind and selfless. And he's my favorite person in the world."

That was exactly when the door of the sail loft swung open. Matt stepped out. We all turned toward him, a back-pack full of who knows what—probably stolen sail designs—slung over one shoulder and a furtive glance around before his attention caught on me.

"What are you doing here?" His eyes sparked with anger, and he scanned the area.

"Great. Just what we need. Another murderer," I sobbed before I could catch myself. Asher's gaze met mine in question. "Oh, you weren't there when we figured it out. Matt killed Captain. He stole the designs for his sails."

"Wait. How'd you know that? Who are you talking to?" Matt's angry eyes flashed around, not seeing the ghosts I did. "Are you the one who called the police? You meddling …" He didn't finish that sentence, instead pulling out a knife. "I'll teach you to stick your nose where it doesn't belong."

He came at me in a flash, so fast I couldn't even blink, let alone move.

A chill ran through me as Matt approached, the hand with the knife slicing down through the air, right for my heart. But just as Matt stabbed downward, Asher's spirit appeared in front of me. I flinched, knowing there were limits to his energy use. He'd tried stopping a bullet for the chief months ago and it hadn't worked. He'd merely deflected the bullet.

He would try everything in his power. I just worried it wouldn't be enough.

I felt a pulse of energy as he made himself as solid as possible. I couldn't see anything through him for a second. And then, Asher grew transparent once more. Matt's knife had stopped a foot from my chest.

I gasped. He stopped it.

Matt scowled. His fingers shook as he let go and stepped back. The knife clattered to the ground. I could see it all happen through Asher as he faded. Not because he wasn't using energy any longer, I realized. Because he was leaving. He'd learned who had killed him and why. His unfinished business was no longer standing in his way. He was passing on.

He turned to me, realizing the same thing as I just had.

A tear crawled slowly down his ghostly cheek, and he reached for me, only to find that his hand was already gone.

"I love you, Rosie. Goodbye." His words were ghosts in and of themselves, fading away.

I could barely see him through the tears in my eyes. "I love you too." I reached forward, but he was gone.

24

At that point in my ghost-seeing life, I'd experienced quite a few spirits move on. They flashed before my eyes in that moment: Grandma Helen, SJ Mills, Maryanne, Cole, the Gilchrists, Scamp, and Dominic.

Each time, no matter how unprepared I'd been to say goodbye, it always felt right. They always seemed happy, ready. I'd hoped it would be the same with Asher, that seeing him leave would give me the same peace I'd experienced with the others.

I'd been fooling myself.

Not only did watching him leave feel like it was ripping my heart in two, but his soul hadn't exuded the same calm energy theirs had. He hadn't been ready. Which just made it all hurt even more.

I don't know how long I stared into the space where he'd been, but it couldn't have been more than a few seconds, because Matt recovered from his shock and started running toward me again, his eyes locked on the knife at my feet.

"Oh, no you don't," Trip called, racing forward and standing in front of me to block him. He sent out a pulse of energy, and Matt flew back like he'd just run straight into a wall.

I kicked the knife behind me. With shaking fingers, I called the chief.

"Rosie, I'm sorry this is taking longer. We can't find Matt and—"

"He's here. He's at the sail loft. Come quick," I blurted, tears wracking my whole body.

"The sail loft? We were just there." Frustration growled through his words. "Okay, we're on our way. Are you hurt?"

I took inventory of my body. My chest felt as though someone had ripped it in two, a cut right where my heart beat inside my rib cage. But it was just emotional pain. Still, it took more effort than I expected to say, "No. I'm fine. Matt's down, but I'm not sure for how long."

"We'll be right there." In the background, I could hear him turn on his sirens and call orders to the other officers.

My shaking hand couldn't seem to hold up my phone any longer, so I ended the call and let the phone drop to my feet. I let my gaze fall with it, closing my eyes to squeeze out the last few tears. The sirens quickly closed in on my location. They really hadn't been far away.

When I looked up, Trip's spirit stood in front of me.

"Go find your friend," I said, noticing he was fading quickly.

He raised a hand in a last goodbye. "Thank you, Rosemary. I'll never forget you."

And then I turned around, seeing Charlie's ghost

standing behind me, arms crossed smugly. Hate overwhelmed me.

"You," I growled, stalking toward him.

But I stopped, remembering there was absolutely nothing I could do.

He cackled as he realized it as well. "Pitiful girl."

"Pitiful?" I spat out the question. "You don't even have enough of a soul to stay in ghost form for more than a few minutes. You've been haunting a building for decades, and you'll be stuck there forever because of what you've done. I'm not the one who's pitiful," I said.

He scowled, and I noticed he was already fading. What little soul he had left was too weak to maintain this spirit form. Looking down at the salt I'd dropped earlier during the commotion. I stooped to grab the container, opened it in one quick movement, and tossed it over him, helping him along.

And then I crumpled into a ball and cried.

That was where the chief found me minutes later when he pulled up, two Astoria police cars screeching to a halt just after his SUV. The uniformed officers ran toward Matt, who was only just coming to after his run-in with Trip.

Raymond came to me, scooping me up into his arms as I sobbed.

"Rosie, honey, are you hurt? Please, you've got to talk to me." His voice shook like only a father's could, one who was worried about his daughter.

I blinked through my tears and looked into his eyes. I uncurled my arms from around my body and showed him I was okay. "I'm not hurt. I promise. Just sad." I cleared my throat. "Scared," I added, knowing the sad part wouldn't make sense.

"She stopped the knife with her mind," Matt was yelling, pointing at me as they shoved him into the police car.

The chief studied me. I used what little energy I had left to roll my eyes. "He just doesn't want to admit that a girl is stronger than him."

Chief Clemenson set me in the passenger seat of his car. "I'll be right back," he said, placing a hand on my cheek. "I'm so glad you're okay."

I covered his hand with mine for a second before he walked away, my love for him mending a tiny piece of my shattered heart.

"I'm going to take my daughter home. You know where to reach me if you need anything. You've got this under control?" I heard him talking to the Astoria police, and then he was back.

Raymond started the car and drove. He must've picked up my phone from where I'd dropped it outside, because he set it in the console between us. I pressed my forehead against the glass, not speaking. Raymond didn't push me to talk, he simply grabbed my hand with one of his and held on tight the entire drive home.

―――――

I MUST'VE FALLEN asleep in the car, because the next thing I remembered was the chief's hand rocking my shoulder.

"Rosemary, we're home." He stood outside the open passenger door and offered me a hand.

I lunged out of the car, pulling him into a tight hug. "Thank you. I love you," I said into his uniform.

He hugged me back. "I love you, too, Rosemary. I'm so lucky to have you as a daughter." He started toward the house, helping me to the door. "Do you want me to come inside?" he asked.

"No, I'm okay." My voice was small. "Callie's inside. Is it okay if I give you my statement tomorrow? I'm completely exhausted."

New as it may have been, the dad part of him won out over the police officer. I could tell by the way his dark eyebrows knit together that he had about a million questions for me, but he let them go, for now.

"Sure. We can talk tomorrow." He gave me a quick nod before heading back to his SUV.

I wondered if he would drive back to Astoria tonight or if the officers there had everything under control without him. I watched him pull away as I stumbled inside. I needed Callie. I searched the tearoom, but it was empty. That was when I saw the back door was open. I walked that way, feeling like a zombie, ambling toward the fresh air.

"Cal, I have something to tell you," I croaked out as I stepped onto the porch. It didn't feel real. Somehow, having to tell her that Asher was gone felt like reliving it all over again.

But Callie wasn't alone on the porch.

She turned from where she sat on the steps with Destiny. Callie's face was red and puffy. Tears streaked her cheeks. She got up and ran toward me.

"I already know," she said as she hugged me tight, almost so tight I couldn't breathe.

Destiny stood.

"You felt it?" I asked her once Callie let go.

The herbal witch nodded.

"Do you always feel it when a spirit moves on?" I asked, not sure why this was important right now, but needing to talk about something.

She shook her head. "Not usually, but when so many pass on at once, it creates a shift."

"So many?" I asked.

Destiny cocked an eyebrow at me. "You cleared up quite a bit of unfinished business tonight, lady."

I turned to Callie. "Genny?"

"Her grandfather came to apologize to her for giving her that locket and the ensuing visions. They passed on together," Callie said.

"Around the same time as Trip and his best friend, I'm guessing ... and Asher," I added, breaking into another round of sobs.

Callie pulled me into another tight hug.

"I'll leave you two alone," Destiny said, placing a gentle hand on my shoulder. "Come see me when you're ready to talk."

My gaze snapped up. "Destiny, the rift up at Watchman's Bluff," I said through a gasp. "The one Meow got caught in a few months ago. You said it's a weak spot in the veil between this plane of existence and the other side. Do you think I could use it to talk to Asher? Just one last time?"

Destiny's mouth pulled into a hopeful smile. "Maybe, hon. If anyone can, it's you and Asher. You two had quite the connection. I've never seen anything like it. Just don't get your hopes up." She blew a kiss.

I knew Destiny was worried about me clinging to something that might not be possible, but it was that hope that would get me through that night, and the next few days. Because despite Destiny's reservations, I'd never been more sure of anything in my life as I was that Asher's soul and mine were connected, forever.

25

_____

Eight days later ...

I studied the charred remains of the tree trunk as the summer wind gusted around me. Watchman's Bluff was blustery on the best of days, but that morning, it felt like I was about to get picked up by a tornado and set down in Oz.

Honestly? I would have welcomed the ride.

Lately, I wanted to be anywhere but in Pebble Cove. It was an odd feeling for someone who loved this town so much. But I wondered if that feeling of home had been so strong because it was where Asher had been. And now that he was gone, everything reminded me of him. I cried when I saw a newspaper, when I stared out at the ocean, when I cracked open a new book.

I just needed to talk to him, if only one last time.

So that was why I'd been sitting there, staring at the rift in the veil, trying everything to call Asher to me.

Destiny had given me rocks to hold while doing so. I'd

gone back to her shop almost daily, hoping she had something new for me to try. Today I held a veritable pile, between the moonstone, rose quartz, and green tourmaline, anything to help strengthen my connection to the spirit world.

"Asher Archibald Benson," I said for the dozenth time, resting my chin on the hand that wasn't filled with gemstones. "I miss you, Ash," I whispered.

A flash of brown fur pulled my attention away from the place where the rift should've been. Meow skittered after a butterfly, his ghostly paws making no difference in the insect's flight pattern as he batted at it.

The former mayor had been joining me at the bluff during my past few visits. He skirted around the place with wary interest, in typical cat fashion. He'd gotten stuck in the rift once and he was understandably cautious of the space around the charred trunk.

As if he could sense my sadness, he abandoned the butterfly and jumped up to rub his face against my leg. I felt a delicate bump on my shin.

My eyes lit up. "Meow!" I smiled down at him. "You just used energy to bump into me."

The ghostly cat blinked up at me happily, continuing his pathway back and forth in front of my legs. He rubbed up against me a second time, meowing proudly.

"Well, if I want to end my time here today on a positive note, I think that's my sign." Sighing, I stood and walked back to my car, needing to start the day and open the tea shop.

Callie had offered to stay, to not move into the bed-and-breakfast. She had a whole schedule worked out with

Georgie and Sam where she would sleep at the tea shop and get up super early to be ready for breakfast service at The Gull's Nest.

But I couldn't accept. She needed to move on with her life, and I knew where to find her if I needed her. Even so, she stayed a few days past what she'd planned, getting me through the worst of my tears. Mom checked on me every day, making sure I was doing okay with the transition—even though she couldn't have known how difficult of a transition it was for me. Still, her presence brought me comfort.

Showing up at my house was still surreal these days. Without Callie or Asher it felt like a different place altogether, like a person I thought I knew but was learning they were the complete opposite of what I'd always assumed.

I went through the motions of the day. It was getting easier. I laughed with the locals, gossiped with Daphne, grumbled with Carl, and served tea while the sun shone down on the glittering waves out my window. I read over the journal entries I'd written during those last few days with Asher, thanking Callie for the idea every chance I got. I had dinner with Mom, Raymond, and Callie, and I'd been out paddleboarding with Jolene and Beck again—though, without Asher's support, I'd fallen in. The fact that I was soaked had helped cover up my brief bout of tears in that instance.

It was still a good life. It just had an Asher-sized hole in it.

That morning in the tea shop I had an especially fun distraction. During my busiest hour, the Rickster and Celeste came in and found a seat. They were dressed to the nines, the Rickster in a black suit and Celeste in a flowing black dress. Right. Captain's funeral had been today. I hoped the Rickster got to say a proper goodbye to his best friend. I knew, now, how important that was.

Luckily, Celeste seemed to be doing a good job of comforting him. Their hands were clasped together, and they stared deep into each other's eyes, like they might die if they were forced to look apart even for a moment. Proving they wouldn't, the Rickster tore his gaze from Celeste and stood, clearing his throat.

My heart swelled as it anticipated a grand romantic speech or equally passionate gesture. I was glad to see that my broken heart wasn't incapable of being happy for other people and their love.

But, as usual, the Rickster surprised us all when he opened his mouth.

"People of Pebble Cove, we've come here today to let you know Celeste is leaving." His wild white hair caught bits of sunlight and almost appeared to glow.

Gasps sounded around the now quiet room.

"I know. It looks like we're head over heels in love with each other." The Rickster held up a hand and peered around as if he'd read everyone's minds, which was fair since he'd definitely plucked the thoughts right out of mine. He gazed down at his ex-wife. "And we are. But we're much better apart than together."

At this, Celeste nodded, giving the Rickster a wink.

"But don't worry. She won't be a stranger around these parts," he continued.

This speech was turning into some kind of old western monologue. I pressed my lips together, fighting the laughter that wanted to bubble out of me. He must've realized things were going off the rails, because he stopped it there, taking a bow before motioning to Celeste, who did the same.

The customers in the tea shop clapped warily, like they were unsure if what they'd just witnessed was real or some kind of surprise dramatic performance. The Rickster spent the next hour showing off the collection of postcards he'd kept over the years from Captain. Based on the amount of *or die* phrases Cap included in his messages to the Rickster, the man hadn't been lying to the chief when he'd said it was something they'd always said to each other.

Compared to the Rickster and Celeste's visit, the rest of my day was completely uneventful. But I was grateful for the routine, the sameness. It meant I didn't have to think too hard, that I could afford to let my mind wander.

It always went to the same place. Asher. I could still see his smile, the way it would travel up to his eyes, making them wrinkle in the corners. I could hear his laugh just as crisply as if I had a recording of it and had it on replay in my mind.

And I could still feel his touch, full of energy and love.

Those were the things that got me through the days.

———

I HAD JUST CLOSED—THE click of the lock and the swipe of the open sign to the closed side were music to my ears. I was ready to have a quiet dinner at home and lose myself in a story. We were reading a fun mystery called *Finlay Donovan Is Killing It* for the book club this month. I was excited to feel the heart-pounding excitement of an investigation. My investigating days felt behind me, somehow. Like an inspector without their sidekick, nothing had the same spark.

I was gathering the last few dirty teapots and mugs from the tables and loading everything into the dishwasher when the back door opened. Wind rushed inside. I frowned. It could be Callie, or Mom, or Raymond. Carl usually knocked, and Daphne only used the front door.

Standing up, I peered over to find Riley standing inside. He surveyed the empty shop.

"Hey, Riley," I stepped out from behind the tea bar, blinking in question.

He wasn't supposed to come by until tomorrow. I'd begged for a rain check last Friday, telling him I wasn't feeling well and had closed the shop for the day—which wasn't a lie. I knew I needed to return his letter, the one Catherine had written to Hannah, but I wasn't sure I was ready to hear whatever it was he'd been trying to tell me last week.

It looked like I didn't have a choice, though. He was here, and I wasn't in a position to turn away any friends.

Riley turned to face me. It hit me then how handsome he was. He wore another one of those outfits that his students thought made him look like a hipster. His face contorted in question at first, then it broke into a big smile that crinkled the edges of his eyes. His blue eyes.

My heart stopped.

Riley didn't have blue eyes. His were brown.

"Ash?" I breathed out the question.

My knees didn't work. I reached out for something to grab ahold of. He raced forward, holding out his hand to steady me.

"Yeah, it's me," he said, smiling down at me.

"You didn't move on?" I asked, feeling my confusion at odds with the absolute happiness bouncing around inside me. "But we solved your murder."

Asher held me tighter. "It wasn't my unfinished business, apparently." He wet his lips.

They shone with moisture. It was then that I registered a faint cinnamon scent and realized the hand that gripped mine was warm.

I sucked in a quick breath, and then I passed out.

26

I came to a moment later in Asher's arms as he carried me into the library and set me on the couch. Eyes fluttering open, I gazed up at him. He knelt next to the couch, leaning over me and smiling down as his dark hair fell forward onto his forehead.

My fingers reached up, sweeping gently across his cheek and catching on the stubble along his jaw. I ran them through his thick hair, much like the night he'd kissed me, but oh so different. I brought my other hand up and cradled his face, smiling as I sat up. Now that I was level with him, I kissed his forehead, then his nose, then my lips met his. They were warm and soft, and I breathed in the cinnamon scent of him that I'd spent so many nights dreaming of.

I sat back, my hands moving to his shoulders, then his chest. My eyes widened. Asher was strong. As if he could still read my thoughts, like the spirit version of him always could, his mouth tugged into a half smile.

I moved to swing my legs off the couch so there was

room for him. He winced as he repositioned himself to sit next to me, placing a hand on his right knee.

When I frowned in question, he said, "I ran into a tree trunk before I realized I couldn't walk through things anymore."

"How is this even possible?" I asked.

Asher shrugged. "Your guess is as good as mine. I woke up just like I usually do after using too much energy, but instead of showing up here, I was up in the woods by The Pines."

I sucked in a breath. "Where you died." Shaking my head, I added, "I've been going to Watchman's Bluff every day, trying to see if I could use the rift in the veil to talk to you. I didn't even think about trying the place where they found your body."

Asher placed his hands gently on either side of my face and planted another slow kiss on my lips. Pulling back, he refocused.

"Thank you. I think I could feel you calling me. Your hope was like a bright, warm light in the darkness. I just kept moving toward it. The next thing I knew, I was coming to like I normally do when I use too much energy, although it wasn't like normal. I felt the wind. I could smell the sea breeze. I was a little cold. I haven't been cold in over a hundred years." He sighed. "But I thought it was just in my imagination, so I tried to transport myself back here, and nothing happened. I walked forward, right into a very solid tree trunk." He flinched.

While he talked, my fingers laced through his, connecting me to him as much as I could.

Suddenly worry engulfed me. It must've shown on my

face because Asher said, "I know. I worried about it being temporary, too, like one last night before I move on for good."

Holding his hand tight in mine, I pulled him up off the couch. "Come with me. We need to talk to Destiny."

Asher nodded, but his gaze flicked toward the kitchen. "Is there any way I can grab something to eat for the road? It feels like I haven't eaten in a century." He laughed.

I did too. "Of course," I said, but my laughter quickly devolved into tears. I pinched the bridge of my nose, willing them to stop.

Warm arms wrapped around me. I sank into them, letting myself listen to the beating of his heart and the breath in his lungs as I cried.

"Hey, what's wrong?" Asher asked.

"It's just too good to be true." I looked up into his blue eyes as his fingers tangled themselves into my hair. "I spent so much time wishing this could happen, and now that it has, I don't know what to do. I'm really worried this is just a dream. Or maybe I made a batch of tea out of the wrong kind of leaves and I'm hallucinating."

He wrapped his arms tighter, tucking me under his chin and planting a kiss on the top of my head. "I guess we'll just have to see what happens. We'll make the best of it, dream or hallucination or not. We have to cherish every second."

He was right. If this was limited, I was wasting precious time. Drying my tears, I pulled him into the kitchen where I had some leftover pizza. I heated a piece in the microwave while he ate one cold.

Asher's eyes went wide as he chewed his first bite. His head rolled back for a second before he took another bite.

"That's the greatest thing I've ever tasted," he said, mouth full.

I cocked an eyebrow at him. "I would say it's because you haven't had food in a hundred years, but I think you're right. Pizza is the best."

He finished the cold piece just as the other was coming out of the microwave.

"Let's take this to go," I said, gesturing toward the car. "Sun City's a long drive. I want to make sure Destiny's still open by the time we get there."

Ash placed one more cold piece of pizza on the plate to take with the warm one.

I grinned at him, beaming in an unbelieving way that made me feel like I was floating. It was the same feeling I had as he climbed into the passenger seat of my car, and that I had each time I glanced over at him as I drove.

"So tell me everything that's happened since I disappeared," he said.

One would expect him to be staring out the windows as I drove, to be taking in the scenery and experience riding in a car, but he kept his eyes locked on to me, like he was worried I might disappear at any second, as though I was the one who'd come back to life.

I told him about Matt's confession in the holding cell at the Astoria police station, how he'd been so upset when Cap fired him that he'd stolen the designs. He found out Captain was going to the Rickster for help with patents, so he hid out in the water in Pebble Cove until he saw him and that's when he stabbed him.

He was the one in charge of sending the Rickster's checks, and he'd stopped, at first because he didn't think the

228

Rickster deserved to still be getting money from the company, but then later because he believed it would look bad for the Rickster, and that he could frame him for the murder.

His mom had lied for him, giving him an alibi. He'd told her that he was at home alone, and the police would waste time investigating him if they knew that. Energy spent looking into him would take away precious time and resources from finding Captain's actual killer. She'd said she had no idea he was the one who'd actually committed the crime.

I explained how Trip moved on, as did Lyle and Genny. And how Callie had moved out.

"She's loving the new job," I told him. "She's already added five new items to the breakfast menu."

Asher leaned back into the seat, relaxing after hearing that. "I'm so glad."

I sucked in a deep breath. "Omigosh, Callie!" I almost pulled the car over. "We should've told her before we left town. She's going to flip out."

Asher held up a hand—a physical, real hand!—and said, "I think it's good that we talk to Destiny first. It would be sad to get her hopes up if I'm only here for a short time."

My mood sobered with the reminder of what could be.

Asher threaded his fingers through mine as I drove.

When I parked in front of Destiny's shop, we both pulled in deep, steadying breaths. Then we entered.

It was about an hour before she closed, but she wasn't behind the register counter when we walked inside. In fact, she wasn't anywhere to be seen. I was about to call out a hello when I heard the faint shuffling sound of cards in the back room. I pulled aside the curtain and found Destiny curled over a table, flipping over tarot card after tarot card, muttering to herself.

"Hey," I said, hoping to snap her out of whatever trance she was in, and hoping it wasn't a magical trance that might be harmful for her to be pulled from—I didn't know. Maybe it was like sleepwalking.

Her gaze snapped up to me. "Oh, Rosemary. Sorry, I'm just trying to …" She squeezed her eyes shut for a second. "I felt something ... a disturbance earlier, and I'm not sure ... just trying to figure out—" She was scattered. Her vision ping-ponged around the small back room.

Until Asher stepped next to me and said, "I think I know what it was."

Destiny blinked like she couldn't trust her eyes, doing a great impression of what I must've looked like earlier.

"You didn't move on?" she asked, repeating my first question to Asher.

Asher's lips arched. "It's so much more than that," he said, reaching forward and taking her hand with his.

She yelped as she touched his skin, like his warm hand had burned her. Then she backed up. "How? Why? How?"

"We were hoping you might know," I whispered.

She snorted. "I have never seen anything like this." Then, as if remembering she was clairvoyant, she stood and paced. "What if your unfinished business was never about your murder?" she mused, much like Asher and I had speculated. "Maybe you were always meant to find true love." She snapped her fingers. "What stones did you have on you when you woke?" She pointed to his pocket.

Asher blinked, patting his pockets. "That's weird. I had a

bunch. The normal ones: jasper, malachite, green tourmaline, rose quartz." His eyes widened as he stopped, holding a hand against his thigh. He reached into that pocket and pulled out a single rose quartz. "This is the only one left."

Destiny's lips curled into a huge smile, the kind you can't hold back even if you try. "Unconditional love. I think you were sent back because of your love for Rosemary. Your last act was giving up all of your energy to save her life. That kind of love has repercussions in the universe."

Asher and I looked at each other.

"That sounds about right," Ash said, gently caressing my cheek.

I leaned into his hand, loving the feel of his skin against mine.

"But we're worried about whether it's permanent or if it's just a consolation prize from the universe for a day or so before he'll have to move on." I turned toward Destiny, frowning to show my concern.

Much to my disappointment, Destiny shrugged. "I can't tell you that. The universe works in mysterious ways." She motioned to Asher. "Obviously. It could be twenty-four hours. You might have a week. You could have a month." She shook her head. "You might have forever." She narrowed her eyes at him, then picked up a pencil from the table and chucked it at Asher's head.

"Ouch." He flinched as it smacked against his forehead and bounced off.

"You can feel pain, which is a good sign. If this body was just temporary, it might be less likely to have feelings." Destiny nodded, satisfied.

Asher rubbed at his forehead. "You could've asked me."

He pulled up the leg of his tweed pants, showing off the bruise he'd gotten from running into the tree in the forest. "I already hurt myself before I realized I couldn't walk through things anymore."

"That's good." Destiny moved her attention to me. "Basically, you've got to treasure every second you have with each other. Treat every day like it's your last, and every morning like it's a new start. The universe works in cycles. I'd say if you make it a full moon cycle, that's a great sign."

Asher snaked his arm around my waist and pulled me close to him as we listened. Destiny waved her hands at us. "Okay, now get out of here. You two are giving me a toothache, you're too sweet." She grinned.

We climbed back into my car and just sat there. I didn't trust myself to drive yet. Silence stretched between us as we digested what we'd just learned.

"I'm going to text Callie to meet me at the house." I clenched my teeth, excitement leaking out of me in a squeal as I pulled up her name in my contacts. But I stopped. "Oh, we should have her meet us at the cannery instead. We have to tell the ghosts too." I turned toward him. "I wonder if you can still see them."

Asher blinked. "Oh, you're right. I guess we'll see." He wet his lips, looking apprehensive for a moment. "You don't think … is it rude to show them?" he asked finally. "I mean, is it going to feel like I'm rubbing it in their faces that I got a second chance?"

My heart warmed. Of course he would be worried about their feelings. I took his hand in mine and squeezed tight. "Ash, they're our friends. They're going to be happy for you."

Nodding, he seemed to exhale the worst of his worries. "Okay."

With that, I texted Callie, telling her to gather the ghosts and meet me at the cannery in an hour. The local group was getting smaller, only comprised of Meow, Lois, Max, and Tim at that point.

Sure. What's up? she texted back almost immediately.

My fingers hovered over my phone screen as I thought of what to say. I settled on, **I have good news. I'll explain everything when I get there.**

Anticipation built inside me as I drove, making me push down harder on the accelerator. Asher's hand settled on my knee, calming me instantly. Right. It wouldn't help anything if we got in a crash now.

I slowed. We fell into easy conversation as I explained the book I was reading for the book club. He laughed and asked questions as I described the plot and my favorite scenes. And before I knew it, we'd arrived safely at the cannery. Callie's car waited in the lot, and I could see lights dancing in the upper windows as darkness descended on the coastline.

Asher wrapped an arm around my shoulder as we walked inside together. He let me walk up the staircase first, everyone's attention cutting over to me as I reached the second floor.

"Hey, so what's the good news?" Callie asked, bouncing on the balls of her feet. She'd been overly attentive and worried about me since that night in Astoria.

"Yeah, what's the big deal?" Lois crossed her arms.

I looked back and nodded to Asher. He climbed the last

few steps and walked onto the second floor. The group inhaled a collective gasp.

"Ash!" Callie raced forward. She opened her arms, and he did too. She tackled him in a hug but when her arms wrapped around him, she gasped again and pulled back. "What?" Her mouth dropped open. Her eyes searched him first, then me. Callie turned to the ghosts. "He's ... he's warm?"

Lois, Max, and Tim raced forward.

Asher chuckled and waved, proving he could still see them. It wasn't a huge surprise. He'd definitely had his fair share of experience with death, more so than even Callie or I did.

"We're not sure how it happened," I said through a light, bubbly laugh. "Destiny isn't either. She thinks maybe it has to do with ..." I stopped, embarrassment creeping up into my neck in hot pulses as I thought about saying it aloud.

But Asher had no such qualms. He pulled me to him. "She's pretty sure it has to do with true love," he said, staring into my eyes with his deep blue ones. Then he planted a kiss on my lips.

Someone sighed, someone clapped, and there was a meow of celebration. And then Callie was wrapping us both into a hug.

We stayed and talked for a while but hadn't brought proper jackets, and it got cold even on summer nights like tonight. We invited Callie to come back to the teahouse with us, but she shook her head, squeezing both our hands as we said goodbye in the parking lot by our cars.

"You two deserve some time to yourselves." She beamed

at us. "But tomorrow, I'm coming over bright and early. We're going to need a plan about what we're going to tell the town, especially Raymond and Kate," she said, giving us a pointed stare.

She was right. I was glad we had Callie on our side to help with whatever story we decided on.

Once we were back at the tea shop, we fell into normal routines. I made a pot of tea, but this time I brought out two mugs. I steeped some of the Sunset blend, knowing it was all I wanted to smell for the rest of my life. Then we took our tea into the library and curled onto the couch together. I laid my legs over his, and his arm wrapped around my back. It was like we were as intertwined as possible.

We talked into the night until we both fell asleep.

27

Thirty-two days later …

Fresh sea air blew through the open bedroom window. Sunlight filtered in through the old lace curtains. I peeled open one eye, then the other, breathing a sigh of relief when I noticed the shock of dark hair on the pillow next to mine.

Asher was still here.

The hold-my-breath, heart-pounding moments before I knew if he was still here or not had started the morning after his first day back. I'd woken up on the couch in the library, wrapped in his arms, my head laying on his solid chest, listening to his heart beat and beat and beat, the most wonderful sound I've ever heard. And he'd remained here every morning since, right next to me when I opened my eyes.

He didn't dare get up before me for fear of making me doubt, even for a second, that he had moved on. Well, there had been *one* morning where I'd cried out in alarm, but he'd run back into the bedroom, having just needed to pee badly enough that he couldn't hold it any longer, and we'd laughed.

Today, however, was a special day. It marked thirty-two wake ups with Asher by my side. Months had thirty-one days at the most, which meant that at thirty-two, we'd officially made it beyond the month mark, an entire moon cycle.

That wasn't all. We'd made it over a lot of other hurdles too.

Callie had helped us sell the story that Asher was an old friend of hers from Portland who needed a job. She'd asked if he could rent out my spare room and work in the tea shop with me. Raymond wasn't too keen on a strange man living in the house with me, but after meeting Asher, and Callie vouching for his character, he calmed down the protective-dad routine. It didn't hurt that we'd been unable to hide our feelings for each other from the start, and that Callie had declared it love at first sight, which wasn't entirely untrue.

I may not have known it back then, but as Asher tells the story of the first day we met, he knew he loved me from the moment he saw me.

Speaking of love at first sight, the townspeople of Pebble Cove adored Asher. They couldn't stop commenting about how he *just fit right in* and *seemed like he'd lived here his whole life*. Only Daphne had made a fuss about how much Asher looked like Riley, but no one else had spent enough time with Riley—or studied him with the intensity that Daphne had—to tell how close the two really looked.

And it wouldn't be a problem, either, since Riley had moved away a couple of weeks ago.

After canceling on him twice, I finally made the trip out to Sun City to return his letter and hear what he needed to tell me. His sparse decorations were gone, replaced by moving boxes. As it turned out, Riley wasn't a minimalist. He was moving.

He'd gotten a job offer at a university in California the day before I showed up asking about the letter. That was the news he'd been trying to tell me. He was excited about what he called his "dream job" and had moved shortly after Asher showed up. We hadn't had to worry about any awkward encounters with the two men who looked so alike.

Mom had been our biggest hurdle. She'd quirked her eyebrow at his name the first time I'd introduced them.

"Asher?" she'd said, glancing at me.

I'd acted like I didn't know why she would find that odd. "Asher Winters," I said. We'd decided to have him use his mother's maiden name, since he definitely couldn't be Asher Benson anymore.

She'd watched him like a librarian following a toddler with a sticky chocolate bar through the children's section that whole first evening. But Ash had quickly won Mom over, especially on the days he volunteered at the library. The two of them grew closer each time they discussed books. Asher always came home from the library smiling from ear to ear.

When he wasn't helping Mom, he spent a lot of time working with Beck at their paddleboard rental operation. The two men got along famously, and Asher loved the feeling of doing something that made him feel alive.

And I continued to wake up next to my best friend, next to the man I loved.

On morning thirty-two, I reached forward and ran my fingers gently through his hair. He peeled an eye open, smiling at me.

"Sorry," I whispered. "I didn't mean to wake you."

Frankly, I was surprised that I had. We joked that ever since he'd been given a second chance at life, the man slept like the dead. He'd thought it might be hard to get back into the habit of sleeping after all this time, but he was a natural.

Asher reached up and grabbed my hand, pulling it down to his lips. "Never apologize for waking me to the sight of your beautiful face."

I snuggled closer to him under the covers, relishing in the feel of his body next to mine.

When Destiny first mentioned how we wouldn't be sure how long this could last, how we would need to cherish every moment together, I thought it would be stressful. Living each day, not knowing if it was our last together, sounded like living in constant fear.

But it wasn't like that at all.

It felt like each moment we got together was a celebration, a gift. And we felt grateful for each and every day, every moment.

That wasn't to say we didn't have arguments. As we got out of bed that morning, I was reminded of an ongoing one as I noticed a pair of men's socks laying on the floor. Ash was notorious for stripping off his socks and leaving them about our bedroom instead of putting them in the hamper.

Seeing me eyeing the socks, Asher rolled out of bed and bent to pick them up. His hair stuck up adorably on one side. He tossed the socks into the hamper and then placed a kiss on my head as he walked by.

"Want me to come with to get the bakery stuff from Jolene?" he called from the bathroom as he brushed his teeth.

"Of course," I answered, as I always did. "Want to drive?"

He poked his head into the bedroom, his toothbrush sticking out of one side of his mouth, a bit of toothpaste clinging to his lip. "Srrrrsssly?" he asked around the toothbrush.

I nodded. "You're getting way better."

We'd been practicing his driving in the abandoned parking lot at the cannery. And even though he didn't have a license, I figured he wouldn't get pulled over as long as we stuck to Pebble Cove. If he ever got stopped, I knew the chief of police.

Asher disappeared back into the bathroom, spitting into the sink and running water until he stepped back into the bedroom.

"You know, now that we're past thirty-two days, we can start thinking about a driver's license, social security number, and a birth certificate," he said.

We'd been holding off until we made it past a month, just in case.

"I've been thinking about that." A sly grin pulled across my face. "Luckily, I know a guy who has *a guy* for every situation. And he just so happens to owe me one. A big one."

If anyone knew where to get a fake birth certificate printed, it was the Rickster.

And even though things didn't work out with Celeste like the town might've hoped, he was constantly telling me how grateful he was for the role I played in finding Captain's murderer and clearing his name. I'd told him many times that it had been mostly the chief, but each time the Rickster would just wink at me and give me a sly nod.

"We can keep your same birthday, if you want, but I thought it might be fun to use the day you came back to me." I wet my lips as I watched his reaction.

"I think that's a great idea," he said. "And we should make my birth year twenty-five years ago since I almost made it to my next birthday." He squinted as he thought.

He'd been twenty-four when he'd died the first time. We had to qualify everything in that way lately. The first time. There was the *first time*, and the *second chance*. Though, I had a feeling that as we got used to this life, that constant need to remind ourselves of his second chance would fade.

"Twenty-five," I said thoughtfully. "I never pictured myself in a relationship with a younger man." I waggled my eyebrows at him. At twenty-seven, I wasn't too much ahead of him, but it was fun to tease, especially since Asher technically had a hundred years on me.

He laughed, his blue eyes shining. "Have I told you lately that I love you?" He wrapped his arms around me.

"Every day," I said, snaking my arms around his neck. I leaned up to kiss him.

"And I'll never stop."

"For all eternity," I said.

Not ready to say goodbye?

This novella, set after *For All Eternity-tea*, will follow Asher and Rosemary as they head to the big city to meet with the Rickster's *birth certificate guy*.

Releasing in 2023, this novella will be exclusive to members of Eryn Scott's newsletter for the first month, and then will only be available in the final Pebble Cove box set after that.

Sign up for the newsletter now so you don't miss out!

ALSO BY ERYN SCOTT

Mystery:

The Pepper Brooks Cozy Mystery Series

Pebble Cove Teahouse Mysteries

The Stoneybrook Mysteries

Whiskers and Words Mysteries

Women's fiction:

The Beauty of Perhaps

Settling Up

The What's in a Name Series

In Her Way

I Pick You

Romantic comedy:

Meet Me in the Middle

ABOUT THE AUTHOR

Eryn Scott lives in the Pacific Northwest with her husband, two cats, and a dog. She loves classic literature, musicals, knitting, and hiking. She writes cozy mysteries and women's fiction.

Join her newsletter to learn about new releases and sales!

www.erynscott.com

Printed in Great Britain
by Amazon